SHADOWS FROM THE HORIZON

SHADOWS FROM THE HORIZON

Susan N. Namfukwe

WESTBOW
PRESS®
A DIVISION OF THOMAS NELSON
& ZONDERVAN

WestBow Press books may be ordered through booksellers or by contacting:

WestBow Press
A Division of Thomas Nelson & Zondervan
1663 Liberty Drive
Bloomington, IN 47403
www.westbowpress.com
1 (866) 928-1240

ISBN: 978-1-9736-7039-1 (sc)
ISBN: 978-1-9736-7038-4 (e)

Print information available on the last page.

WestBow Press rev. date: 08/14/2019

ACKNOWLEDGMENTS

I wish to acknowledge one very important person Mr Alfred Muyawa **(Bo Fuledi)** my lecturer, Kasiya Business College. This book would not have been without his input. I shall forever remain indebted to him. Lisa thanks for believing in me.

DEDICATION

To my two boys Wila and Noel, my biggest fans!

1

It started like a normal day. The mountains looked blue and green at a distance. The birds were singing, and their songs could be heard above the blowing wind. The sun at the horizon looked big and red like the heaven's smile. The leaves were swinging to the wind in unison. Everything looked peaceful.

Suddenly, there was a loud sound of a bell—*ring-ring, ring-ring*—disturbing the peaceful new born morning.

Mwaka stirred in her bed. She had been awake for a long time but had closed her eyes in deep thoughts, lost in her own world, until the sound of the bell brought her back to reality. She looked at her watch it was exactly 05:00 hours in the morning. She had to wake up and start preparing for the day.

She reluctantly got off from her blankets, wrapped a wrapper around her see-through nightdress, and walked over to the next bed where her friend was sleeping, oblivious to the time. She had folded herself so tightly like she did not want anything to disturb her. Her hands covered her face and was busy snoring. There was now so much commotion around as all the other students had woken up preparing to start their daily routine. Dormitory 9 was usually called the noisiest dorm of all the fifteen dormitories. This was because this is where most of the students who were in their final school grade resided.

"Njavwa," she called as she shook her friend. "Njavwa, wake up"

Her friend turned and opened her eyes.

"The morning bell has gone off, let's go take a shower or else we will be late for breakfast"

"What's the time?" she asked, yawning.

"It's now 05:15 hours. Hurry up, we will be late for breakfast," she repeated.

Breakfast was always served at 06:15 hours. It was taken so early to allow learners have ample time to prepare for classes which began immediately after 07:00 hours every morning. Being late for breakfast was not tolerated because if anyone went anytime later than the stated time, they would find the dining room doors closed and that meant no breakfast for latecomers.

Njavwa threw off the blankets, and stretched like she wanted to break herself in two and commented "It's like I just slept a few minutes ago, ha… nowadays, nights have become so short. I don't get to finish my sleep anymore…."

Her friend who knew her very well didn't respond but just smiled because Njavwa always complained of never having enough sleep every single day. She could sleep for the whole week without waking up if given a chance. Njavwa simply enjoyed her sleep. She looked around as if she had lost something then she remembered where she had put her bathing towel. She grabbed the towel and jogged to join her friend in the shower room. She knew time was of essence in the morning.

Dormitories were divided into compartments, and each dormitory had twelve compartments that accommodated two people. Njavwa and Mwaka shared a compartment, and they almost shared everything.

In the shower room, they found Lucy and Hilda, their classmates also taking their morning shower and a lot of other girls. The school now was a hive of activity as other girls were busy doing their morning chores while others could be seen roaming around in preparation for the day.

Hilda and Lucy exclaimed their good mornings to the two girls and went about splashing water on themselves. Njavwa who did not like taking cold showers reluctantly joined her friends.

"Look at Nja," shouted Lucy, the most talkative girl. Lucy liked talking and could stop at nothing till her audience started departing one by one. She didn't sensor what came out of her mouth and sometimes people could not make any sense out of her talk. She continued, "looking like a mad ghost especially when she's just from sleeping. Look at the scary eyes." They all looked at her and burst into giggles.

"Enough," interrupted Njavwa, who was getting irritated. Today she was just in no mood for useless jokes and especially from Lucy. She wondered if Lucy ever took time to listen to herself. Hilda, who was about to leave the shower room, paused in the doorway as if she remembered something and exclaimed, "Guys today is Mail Wednesday. I am hoping to receive a letter from home." Wednesday was a favourite day for the girls because it was a day they were allowed to receive mail from their homes. The school being in the rural area of the country had very limited network for mobile communications. The only reliable form of communication was through letters which were only distributed once a week on Wednesday. Naturally everyone looked forward to Wednesdays hoping to receive mail from loved ones.

Mwaka and Njavwa looked at each other and continued washing.

"Njavwa, do you think you will receive a letter today?" asked Mwaka thoughtfully, breaking the silence.

"What makes you think I can receive today?" retorted her friend.

"Njavwa, I am just assuming. What's wrong with you today, so touchy..!"

"You know very well that no one writes to me, so what's your problem."

Mwaka looked at her friend pensively and didn't bother to respond and started singing; sometimes she couldn't stand her moody friend.

Njavwa closed her eyes and prayed silently. *Lord, let my mum remember me today, and has my sister forgotten about me too?* These were the only people who wrote to her.

"Mum, why can't you find me a school place in Ndola. There are so many schools around, I don't want to go to a boarding school" she complained, hoping her mother would budge.

"Njavwa, you are behaving like a kid, you are sixteen years old for crying out loud! There are a lot of girls in boarding schools and way younger than you," her mother responded nonchalantly. Njavwa knew her mother was right, especially that she had to repeat two grades along the way, she was about three years older than normal age for her grade.

She also knew that once her mother's mind was set, there was no turning back. She missed her father in instances like this. She knew her father would never allow any of his children to be sent away from home for whatever reason. He loved to say families who grew together stayed together. But since his demise, alot of things had changed. They had to make adjustments to so many things. Her mum had taken over the role of making decisions for "everyone's good" as she would say! Since "Her Majesty" had decided that Njavwa should go to a boarding school, Njavwa had no choice but to make the most of whatever lay ahead of her.

But that was three years ago.

The first day in class, she noticed this girl with big bulgy eyes who used to sit in the back row. Her eyes were so big that when she looked at you, it was like she was seeing through you. She had long kinky, natural hair, and when she's walking, one could actually tangibly see confidence oozing out of her as she walked over to where Njavwa was seated.

"Well, am Mwaka, what's yours?"

"Njavwa," she replied timidly.

"Where are you from?"

"Ndola."

"Oh! I am from the capital city of Zed. Hope you can guess where that is"

And she passed her, swinging her body, leaving Njavwa stunned. She had never seen such insolence! From that day, Njavwa developed an instant hatred towards that girl and said to herself "*Just because she comes from Lusaka doesn't make me any less superior to her.*"

Njavwa remembered her mum's lessons before coming to the boarding school, to never let anyone trample on her or make her feel less important. Her mum emphasized the need for her to learn how to stand on her feet. Njavwa told herself to never accept to feel intimidated in her life.

At first sight, Njavwa appeared to be a quiet and reserved girl. One would mistake her for a timid and shy girl. But once you got to know her, you would discover that she was actually a volcano waiting to erupt. She was very strong-willed and talkative person. She had a stubborn character and could stand up to anybody. Njavwa didn't like to be in the background or to feel intimidated. The strong desire in her to be noticed pushed her to do daring and crazy stuff at times. Therefore the similarities between her and Mwaka aroused the lioness in her, which wanted to dominate above her friend.

From that day henceforth, they were ever at loggerheads. Whatever one said, the other would oppose. They started competing in tests, clothes, fashion, and never said a kind word to each other.

One day, Njavwa was sitting along the corridors, chatting with her friends, when she noticed Mwaka walking towards them. She got up, took a bucket, went to the nearest tap and started to draw water. Immediately Mwaka drew near; Njavwa pretended to be cleaning the bucket and threw the water in Mwaka's direction. Mwaka was outraged. She charged towards Njavwa, grabbed her in the dress and screamed

"What did you do that for, eh?"

"I did not see you, okay! It was an accident. Now let go of my dress", Njavwa answered, unperturbed.

"Why did you pour water on me?' she asked again with water dripping down her dress. Everyone around looked in amazement because they did not know what was happening

"I told you it was an accident, so what do you want me to do….." She responded cheekily. Before she could finish the sentence, a slap landed on her face, and a fight ensued. The headgirl came, stopped the fight, and dragged them to the headteacher as fighting in school was prohibited. Panting and breathing like men from a race, they were a funny sight with scratches all over their faces.

The headteacher upon seeing their looks reprimanded them strongly. He informed them that this was not the first time he was hearing about their tussles.

He further warned that next time he will hear anything about them again, he would make sure they were punished severely.

The hatred between the two girls just grew stronger. The punishment did nothing to help the situation but just added fuel to the fire. The next time, Njavwa was coming from having a shower when Mwaka blew sand in her direction. Again, a fight broke.

This time they never got away with it. The headteacher asked them to dig a pit each according to their height. Njavwa who was slightly shorter than Mwaka, made fun of her friend.The punishment did not end there. The headteacher further told them that he would force them to be friends since they did not want to be friends.

"From today onwards," he directed them, "you will be sleeping in the same compartment. You will share a table in class and dining hall, and from today onwards, I want to be seeing you together all the time.

Should I hear any mischief from any of you again, you will be expelled. I hope the medicine I have prescribed for you will work for the better. Goodluck."

Hence, that marked the birth of a strong historical friendship that had ever existed between the two girls.

They realised that they had a lot in common. They had same interests, they loved reading and fashion and both came from Christian homes, and above all, they both didn't have their fathers. Mwaka had never known her real dad. She had grown up knowing her stepfather as her dad as her mum had separated with her real dad before she was born. Njavwa's dad had died when she was very young and was being raised up by her mother. The people who saw them afterward couldn't believe that these were the same girls who never wanted their paths to cross. Just like the saying that after a storm comes a calm, so it was for the two girls. Everyone congratulated the head teacher for the wise decision he had made to bond the two girls. These girls were always together; whenever you see one, be sure to see the other one nearby as they never left each other at all.

They became simply inseparable.

Later in the day, Njavwa saw Lucy running toward her screaming."Nja! Nja!" as she was fondly called."Guess what! You have received two letters!" she shouted waiving the letters in the air.Njavwa could not believe it."What…..! Who has written to me?"

When she checked the handwriting on the envelopes, she could not help shrieking, "this one is from my mother and this one from my sister,!"

She screamed and skipped with excitement.

"You see. I told you that you will receive mail today", Mwaka remarked with a twinkle in her eye, "Open them we see what mum has written"

"I will, I will, first, let me dance first." She bubbled.

Receiving mail always excited the students because at least it made them feel remembered by their loved ones. It also broke the monotone of school routine, which made the girls always look forward to Wednesdays. Mobile phones were strictly forbidden at the school. There was no way of talking to the outside world on the phone. What was allowed and encouraged was letter writing. This the management of the school thought would encourage students not to forget their letter writing skills which was emphasized as the one of the most important skills to harness. This made most of students to anxiously wait for Wednesday as it was the only day they could hear from their families.

Lucy and Mwaka looked at each other as they watched Njavwa jump up and down. At last she stopped after she had run out of breath. She sat down, sighed, and said, "Mum has remembered me at last. I am so happy." As if her mum ever forgot about her!

Little did she know that those letters would turn her world upside down.

2

Samuel Kabwe was a big businessman of his time. In his mid thirties he had chains of successful businesses countrywide. His friends used to say that he had a 'Midas touch' because whatever he touched turned to gold. He attributed all that purely to luck because some deals he pulled through shocked even him. It is said that some people succeeded because they were destined to, but Sam succeeded because he was determined to. He had acquired properties in almost every part of the country. Not to mention the massive mansion in which he lived. Unfortunately, he had no one to share his wealth with except for his maids and house helps and other privileged employees who helped to look after his properties.

Samuel had everything he dreamed of and all that money could buy except for a wife. However, he never lacked in that area because if he wanted a girl, all he could do was just raise a finger.

Samuel was good-looking, medium height with a stout figure. He had a broad handsome face with big round eyes. Sam was very conscious about his appearance that's why he took time to invest in the state-of-the-art gym in his basement at home. Everyday he spent his first two hours of the morning in the gym.. The worst thing about

Sam was that he knew he was handsome, and he didn't need anyone to tell him that.

Since he divorced with his wife about ten years ago, he vowed never to marry again. Sam didn't live like a saint and never pretended to be one. He wanted to live life like there was no tomorrow. *'Enjoy life today, tomorrow will take care of itself'* 'was his motto and said people who brooded over life were fools.

One thing Samuel didn't want was to become emotionally involved with any girl after his failed marriage. Despite that, most of the times he would secretly wish he had a wife and family around him. He wondered if he would ever find a woman to settle down with again.

There was one incident that had happened, which had been disturbing his mind; he was never at peace whenever he thought about it. Up to now he did not understand what was so special about the young schoolgirl he gave a lift on one of his business trips to Lusaka. He never in his life picked school girls, but whatever prompted him to give a lift to that small girl, even he did not understand. She did not look so young though; she must have been nineteen or maybe twenty-one, he calculated. But just thinking about it made him uncomfortable.

It was on a Monday morning in the month of May, five months had passed, but he still vividly remembered every detail. He saw a young girl standing by the roadside with two large bags. He thought that it would do no harm by giving a beautiful girl a lift. At least he could have someone to talk to whilst driving. He stopped the car, rolled down his window, and said in his charming voice, "Hi beauty, where are you headed to?"

"Am going to Mkushi," she answered. Mkushi is a district in the rural outskirts of the country.

"Mkushi! This is your lucky day. Can I give you a ride? Will drop you off at the next town then from there you can connect."

Njavwa hesitated because she was not sure if she could get a lift from a stranger, especially that he was alone. She was hoping to get a lift from the car that had passengers. He looked harmless anyway. She thought, "*I will save on my pocket money for school.*

Her mum had dropped her at the bus station to catch the school bus. Since she was rushing for a meeting at her work place she had left Njavwa to board a bus by herself. Immediately her mum had left the station, Njavwa decided to go and hitch hike by the road side since she was trying to save as much pocket money as possible. Hitch hiking was usually considered to be cheaper than using ordinary buses. She was confident her mum will have no idea how she would travel as long as she arrived safely.

Njavwa accepted a lift from the stranger. "You said you are going to Mkushi what's there?' Samuel asked.

"I am going to a boarding school, I am at Mkushi Girls School."

"Oh really, what grade are you in? "*She doesn't look like a school girl*, he thought to himself. Njavwa was 19 years old but she looked way older than her age because of her chubby body nature.

"I am in my last grade…," she responded.

"Oh, by the way,since you and I will be together for a while, why don't we get to know each other. I am Samuel Kabwe, but you can call me Sam," he introduced himself.

Njavwa could not believe her ears. So this was the man alot of girls talked about. *The famous Sam…* She couldn't help commenting, "I have heard so much about you..!"

He smiled and said, "Oh, you seem to know me, then we are not complete strangers after all, aren't we!" He didn't even proceed to ask her name and continued chatting about other things.

He coaxed her to go with him to Lusaka and said he would drop her at her school on his way back. The temptation was so strong, but Njavwa could not help thinking about what would happen if her mother found out. And being a Christian, her conscience started ringing, and whenever she felt like that, she knew it was a warning sign. Her conscience was like a GPS. Immediately she was about to go off track, it would start beeping. She knew all the indications. However, she ignored the signs and succumbed to the temptation. After all, she had never been to Lusaka. This was the opportunity to see the famous capital city. And who would find out? *"I am sure everyone will understand that I am just trying to be adventurous,"* she consoled herself.

She proceeded with him to Lusaka where they stayed at a famous five-star hotel for two days. She could not believe the luxury she found herself in. She never, in her wildest dreams, imagined such luxuries existed. He bought her lots of gifts and gave her a lot of spending money to spoil herself at luxurious shopping malls around Lusaka. She felt like she was in wonderland.

The man surely knew how to make a girl feel special, and he made sure he spoiled her.

He was flashing his money like he just picked it from trees!

Sam finally finished his business venture and true to his word on his way back to Ndola, as per his promise, he diverted to Mkushi to drop her at school. He introduced himself to the school headteacher as Njavwa's uncle and handsomely bribed him so that the girl could not be punished as she was late by a week.

That girl…He tried to remember her name only to realise that he did not know her name. All the time he was with her, he only called her Beauty, so he never bothered to find out what her real name was. She was often on his mind! He could not resist the urge to give her a surprise visit. But how was he going to ask for her? He didn't know her name, and no uncle forgets the name of her niece. All he knew about her was that she was doing her last grade!

"What's wrong with me, have I fallen in love? Why am I thinking so much about that little girl?" He couldn't answer those questions.

He therefore decided to discard the idea of visiting the girl before he made a fool of himself before the headteacher.

Samuel had a lot of friends most of them business colleagues. Among his friends he had a very good friend whom he had not seen in a long time. He thought of visiting him just to check up on him. John Phiri was a managing director of a big parastatal company in Ndola. He has been heading that institution for many years. John and Sam were very good buddies from way, way back in their secondary school days and went to the same university afterwards. Apart from just being friends, they were also tribal cousins, which gave John rights to chide his friend anyhow he liked.

After completing their education, John had proceeded to join the workforce in the public sector while Samuel took a totally opposite different route and joined the private sector. They all seemed to be doing fine in the particular professional paths they had taken. That was why once in a while they would meet to reminisce on their lives. They would discuss their professions, business, and even sometimes their private life. Though to Samuel, private life was not an open forum for discussion.

John was married to a beautiful wife and had three handsome boys. Whenever he met with Sam, he never forgot to encourage his friend to consider settling down again. John did not approve of his friend's lifestyle and would often remind him that family was an important aspect of a human's life and that he was not getting any younger. However, Samuel would try to shoot down the serious topic by pretending he was fine the way he was, though deep down, he knew he wasn't.

When Sam entered John's office, the face of the secretary struck him. It was the first time he was meeting her and wondered where the old secretary had gone. The face, it reminded him of something or someone…he stood still for a second trying to recollect but he could not figure out what.

He decided to talk to her. "How are you, madam, you look familiar, have we met before?"

"I don't think so," Evelyn replied smiling.

That smile! "I am Samuel Kabwe."

"And I am Mrs. Siame," she replied. He didn't seem to catch the emphasis on *Mrs.*

The name though didn't mean anything, but he liked the woman instantly. She was beautiful quite all right, but she reminded him of someone. He resolved to find out more about her.

"Can I please see John?"

"You may go right through, he's expecting you," she said, ushering him in. Sam walked into John's office and found his friend working on his laptop. He looked serious, but when he saw Sam, he eased off from what he was doing, and his face brightened up.

"Sam! So nice to see you. How are you?" exclaimed John.

"I am fine, my friend. But look at you, you have really bulged. what's your wife feeding you with? You are growing round and round, can you please mind your belly!"

"Which belly..," laughed John. "Just bring me more food if you can."

"Shut up." Samuel hushed his friend. "You want your pretty secretary to think a respectable person like me carries nonsense."

"So what, as if that's not true." And they both burst into laughter.

One of the reasons Sam liked John most was because he made him laugh, and he felt relaxed whenever he was with him.

"So…," started Samuel. "…How is your wife and the boys?"

"They are very fine, my friend. Infact the other day, my wife was asking about you. When did you get back from your business trip?"

"A couple of days ago. Anyway, I just dropped by to see how you are doing. By the way, why don't we have a few drinks together in the evening?"

"No problem, yes, we need to catch up. That's why I like you, Sam." John was happy. Knowing his friend, a few drinks meant tons and tons of beer and he just couldn't wait.

John didn't understand how his friend managed to spend so much without complaining. He was so carefree, he secretly wished he could be like him but he knew he couldn't with all the responsibilities he had.

Evelyn Siame was a natural beauty. She was a very light person with a figure every girl would die for. She was a person with very few words and had no friends. She had a likeable character which made many people get attracted to her however, she was not a sociable person and she liked it that way. Evelyn had three children, two girls and a boy, who were solely her dependants. She was a widow; her husband had passed on about ten years ago. Her meager salary could barely allow her to meet the needs of her small family, which put her under so much stress most of the times. She wanted the best for her children but she could not afford to give them the life she wanted. It was a big struggle for her just to provide for the needs of her three demanding children. Especially her teenage eldest daughter at a boarding school who had demands which had no limit! But she never complained.

Whenever she thought of her eldest daughter, Evelyn's heart warmed up. She simply loved her. She was her favourite child and especially that she had taken her almost exact looks. She used to see herself in her a lot. Sometimes she felt guilty that she loved one child more than the others." I am not the only one. Don't all parents love one child the best?" she would comfort herself. She couldn't wait for her child to complete her high school education."*I will give her everything she would ask for,*" she promised herself and she prayed earnestly for her each and every night.

Evelyn, in her thirties, was still very beautiful and looked young for her age. Since her husband passed away, she had vowed never to have another man in her life again. She wanted to remain single for the rest of her life. Through the passing years, her vow never weakened, though at times she felt lonely. Her priority was to be with the children and see to it that they grew up in a godly way. She wanted to be the best example to them. However, it was not easy to keep men at a distance. A day hardly passed without her receiving attention from men, but no matter how tempting and handsome they were, she made it clear that she was not interested. She respected her boss, John Phiri, for not taking advantage of her because almost all men she worked with had in one way or another made passes at her.

That man who came to the office today, the way he was looking at her made her heart shudder. He made her feel so small. She had never felt like that in a long time, and that voice…

That day, she decided to walk home slowly to be a company to her own thoughts. She was so engrossed that she did not realise the distance she had covered. She was walking very slowly only to be disturbed.

"Mrs. Siame, I was saying how are you?"

She lifted her eyes and saw her neighbour Mrs Banda, and her face lit up.

"Mrs. Siame, are you okay?" she continued."I started greeting you a while ago, but you could not hear me, so I decided to draw near and find out what's going on."

Feeling embarrassed, she said, "I am sorry, Mrs. Banda, I was lost in my own thoughts. I didn't hear you. Otherwise, I am fine, and how are you. How are the kids?" she asked simultaneously

They are all fine. I am just going to buy bread at the next shop, I will see you later."

"Okay, thanks, bye."And they parted company.

Mrs Banda was a very kind and good neighbor, but Evelyn tried so hard to avoid her because she was a very nosy person. Evelyn had no close friends, she liked her privacy. She had a lot of acquaintances at work and church but no special friend. The only friend Evelyn had was her first daughter, they were very good friends and used to share a lot of things. Since her daughter left to go to a boarding school, she had become very lonely.

"Lukundo, Mum is home," shouted her youngest son to his sister. Ali was always in the habit of announcing the arrival of anyone who entered their gate. He was what you could call a gate announcer, and everyone was used to that. He came running toward their mum and asked, "What have you brought for me?"

"Ali dear, nothing."

"Mama, why?" he asked accusingly."My friends' mums always bring sweets."

"I am sorry, dear, but today, I didn't have money. Come, I will cook you something to eat.

The boy seemed to discern when his mother was not in the mood for talking, so he quietly followed her in the house.

Sam needed to devise a strategy on how he was going to inquire about John's secretary. He didn't know how to start asking because he knew John was not going to take it lightly especially that he disapproved the lifestyle he led. They talked about football since they were all ardent supporters of European football. They talked about politics, the weather, and other general things. But how was he going to start the subject of his secretary? He thought of trying; if he failed, he would use other means.

"John," he started."You have a new secretary, where did you get her?"

"Sam, if it's you, I know where you are heading. Why the interest?"

"Isn't a person allowed to make a genuine comment…? Okay, since you are so touchy…"

"I am sorry, but I just don't trust you…" He continued."Okay, tell me, what do you want to know about my beloved secretary?"

Sam couldn't believe it would be as easy as that. He felt encouraged.

"Do I know her husband?"he queried

"She's a widow," answered his friend nonchalantly.

"A widow! Did you say a widow!" He couldn't believe his ears.

"Sam, I don't want you to add her to your line of conquests. She's a nice lady, and you don't deserve her," said his friend seriously.

But it never ended there. It was such a relief to hear that she was a widow. Sam never slept that night strategizing on how he was going to approach her.

The following day, he deliberately went to John's workplace again after lunch and pretended he was waiting for John and started to chat with her. At last, he announced that he had an important appointment somewhere; he would come to see his friend the following day. Before leaving, however, he remarked that it was so hot and asked her if she wouldn't mind a drink. She jokingly accepted, thinking he was just kidding, but a shock awaited her. Two hours later, a man arrived with a big parcel.

"Are you Mrs. Siame?" he asked.

"Yes, may I help you?"

"Yes, please, I have been sent to deliver this to you."

Before she could find her voice to ask, the man had left. She thought the man had made a mistake but the big box was addressed to her. She decided to check the contents of the parcel. She could not believe her eyes. A note on top of the drinks re-laid her doubts. It read,

Sorry I did not ask you what drink you take. But please accept my small gift. I hope you will enjoy the drinks. Sam

Is this what he called nothing? This man is crazy, she thought. The box had all types of expensive branded liquor, assorted wines, brandies, and whiskies and assorted juices. She was dumbfounded. There were so many drinks that if she wanted she could have opened a liquor store instantly. She called out to Mr. Phiri to come and see what his friend had sent her. He came, saw the drinks, and shook his head without saying a word. Knowing his friend, that was the least he was capable of doing when he was after something.

Perturbed, Evelyn had a sleepless night that day. Little did she know that Sam also spent half the night in the gym because he could not find any sleep. He was restless. It was like there was a string that had tied them up, and was controlling their minds. They were all troubled trying to figure out what was happening to them. Both had vowed never to be involved with any person after their life tragedies. And they both could not control their feelings for once. Sam thought that perhaps after getting what he wanted from Evelyn, she would get out of his system; Evelyn on the other hand thought that she was just moved by the parcel of drinks she had received. In their hearts they both knew that there was something more. The wind outside continued to blow, disturbing the stillness of the night.

The following day, the restlessness from home followed Sam at work. He could not concentrate on his work. The woman he met yesterday was torturing his mind. He decided to go and see her but didn't have the courage to enter the building. He drove back to his office, tried to find something to occupy his mind, but could not. His secretary saw her boss restless that day; it was not like him but thought it better not to ask because whenever Sam had an issue, he would discuss it with the secretary. So she decided to wait until he opened up himself.

Again, Sam thought of going back to see Evelyn. Time was nearing close of business, so he just left the office without announcing where he was going. He reached the offices, parked his car, but failed to draw enough courage to enter the building. As he was pondering of what to do next, he saw Evelyn emerging out of the building the building. He acted as if he was about to leave and called out a greeting to her. She turned, recognized him, and walked toward him.

They exchanged pleasantries, and as she bade him good-bye, he said, "Infact, I was also just leaving. I had come to do something in that next building," he lied. "Would you mind a lift?"

"It's fine. I will get on public transport. ' I need to buy some stuff in town before I get home." She turned down the offer politely

He produced that special smile and said, "I don't mind taking you wherever you are going, but please just allow me to give you a lift. I insist."

She could not refuse. She politely thanked him and got in the latest jeep he was driving that day.

Once she was settled, she coughed and started. "By the way, Mr. Kabwe." He wished she would stop calling him that. "Honestly, I don't know how to thank you for the drinks."

"Oh dear, you make it to sound as if I bought you an aeroplane, that was nothing. Mind if we stop by and get a few more drinks?" he said, looking serious.

"Uhmm, no thanks, I still have enough at home."

He looked at her and grinned.

"Okay, next time, not so." They looked at each other and both smiled. Suddenly they all became pensive; each became lost in their own thoughts. The silence that enveloped them could be touched.

3

Njavwa could not understand what she was feeling after the excitement of the letters had died down. She took the letters and decided to read her sister's first and then end with her mother's.

Mwaka came, looked at her friend holding a letter, and commented, "You mean you haven't read the letters up to now?"

She answered nonchalantly, "No, but that's what I am doing right now."

There was nothing much in her sister's letter, only that she missed her very much and that her mother had started dating a certain rich man who had bought them a lot of stuff …

> *You will come and see him, and I think you will like him*
> *because we all do. Ali is sending his greetings, and you know*
> *that I love you so much. Lukundo*

Njavwa smiled; her sister was so sweet. The letter brought a lot of memories. Her mum dating…? What changed? She wondered. She put the letter on her chest, and tears freely flowed down her face. Mwaka who was resting on her bed saw her friend shedding tears and said, "You know, the problem with you, my friend, you are too emotional! Let me see what your sister has written."

Njavwa passed the letter to her

"Aren't you reading the other one?"

"Not this time."

"I wish Ricky could write to me," Mwaka went on."Can you imagine that from the time I wrote to him, he hasn't replied to my letter ?" Ricky was Mwaka's boyfriend.

Njavwa replied " Sometimes I envy you. I wish I also had a boyfriend. Imagine a big girl like me without a boyfriend?"

"Njavwa!, what about that big uncle you met on your way here?"

The girls hit their hands and giggled at the same time.

"Mwaka, please, don't ever mention that. That man is old enough to be my grandfather, so please, never should you mention him again. I want to forget that I met him."

Njavwa remembered how her friends used to tease her that she was still a virgin. It never used to bother her because she knew who she was. Being a Christian, she believed that she could only have sex only when she got married. In fact that's what her mother always emphasized to her all the time. The fact that she was nineteen years old with no boyfriend troubled her at times, but she never wavered her trust in her faith. Nevertheless what she did on her way to school haunted her, especially that the man was old enough to be her dad! What happened to the principled Njavwa! She felt cheap and regretted the incident.

The guilt of what she did never left her. What would her mum say if she knew what she had done? She had betrayed her mum's trust and even her own because she had so much faith in herself. She thought she could never sleep with a man just like that…She didn't want to think any more about it, but she could never forget the incident no matter how hard she tried. It was printed on her memory. The times she had tried to confide in Mwaka, she would console her that she liked worrying too much for nothing."Live life,Njavwa, that is life."

4

"Thanks for the ride," exclaimed Evelyn.

"Anytime my dear". Sam replied quickly and continued. "So this is where you stay. You have a nice house, he complimented. I am doing some construction works, and I am checking different house plans. Would you mind if I had a quick look at your house?" he lied; he just wanted to spend a little more time with her.

"No problem you can come in." She led him inside "Ali…Ali," she shouted. "Please come and greet the visitor."

Meanwhile, Sam was busy checking the photographs in the picture flames stuck on the wall. He saw a handsome man whom he concluded was the late husband and pictures of three kids everywhere in the house. The resemblance of the eldest of the three children with the mother was so striking. This family reminded him of something, but he still didn't know what.

Suddenly, a small boy of about seven years emerged.

"Please come and greet Uncle…"

"Sam," he added. "You are a handsome boy. Whom do you resemble?" he asked while swinging the boy's hand.

"Mum tells me that I look like my dad," he answered shyly Then as if he remembered something, he turned and pointed to the picture on the wall. "There, look that's my dad …"

Evelyn who was silently watching from a distance, amused, interrupted, "Ali, where's your sister?"

"She escorted her friend from the yellow house."

"So you mean you are home alone?"

"Yes mummy" he responded still holding Sam's hand.

Sam developed an instant liking to the boy. He found himself commenting, "You're a nice boy."

While looking at his mother.

Evelyn responded with a smile. She took Sam around the house, but she noticed that the person she was showing the house wasn't looking interested and just wondered what it was about. They chatted for sometime then he rose to go. Before he could say his good-bye, Ali said, "Uncle, Mum showed me how to make tea. Do you want me to make some for you? Can I Mum?" he said looking for his mum's approval.

Evelyn did not know what to say. She was stunned and embarrassed that she did not offer the visitor anything. She apologized. Sam was, however, very delighted to stay for tea. Evelyn went to the kitchen to make tea as she promised Ali that he would do the honors of making tea next time.

When she came back in the living room, she found Sam and Ali getting along pretty well joking and laughing. They had tea together, and finally he rose to go. He thanked Evelyn and Ali for the warm hospitality.

"Please allow me also to return the favour by taking you out to dinner on Saturday. Don't refuse, I will be greatly honored." Sam said with his big eyes looking serious.

Evelyn tried to give excuses but could not succeed. They say a good deed deserves another, and so it was set.

Ali was so excited that he started singing about it every day. He just couldn't wait for Saturday especially that their mum could not afford to take them out for meals.

At last, Saturday slowly finally came. By 19:00 hours, they were all ready and set to go. Their mother, clad in a dark sleeveless dress, dangling earrings, and a gold chain on her neck, looked dashing. Her hair was nicely tied on top of her head. She looked beautiful even her children had not seen their mum looking so stunning in a long time. Evelyn, in her heart, was wondering why she had taken so much trouble to look good and to dress with care. She knew she wanted to look beautiful, and she was satisfied with herself that her efforts had paid off.

At exactly the stated time, the car hooted outside the gate announcing the arrival of Sam.

Sam held his breath when he saw Evelyn coming with the children. The girl looked slightly like her mother, but his eyes wanted to rest on their mother. He vowed to himself never to let this woman go no matter what it would cost him. He opened the doors for them and remarked, "You look stunning."

She acknowledged his compliment and blushed like a schoolgirl. Evelyn was thankful that it was dark and Sam could not see her blushing face. It was a long time since any man had told her that.

All the way to the plush restaurant, Evelyn could feel Sam's eyes on her, but she pretended not to see. They were welcomed by a tall smiling waiter who ushered them to their table. He handed them the food menu and got their orders. In no time their four course meal was ready. They had meals that they hadn't had in a long time with a live band playing in the background. Evelyn could see young Ali struggling with his fork and knife but Lukundo was at hand in helping his brother. Evelyn was thankful that her children had portrayed their best behavior during the outing. She was concerned that maybe Ali could be out of control. But she marveled at how easily they had adapted to change.

The way Sam was looking at her made her develop goose bumps;

They were interrupted by a waiter who brought them wine to wash down their sumptuous meals and provided dessert for the kids. It was such a memorable time that Evelyn was sure the kids would never forget it. They went home late in the night feeling elated and satisfied. Evelyn was thankful that at least the next day was Saturday and the kids were not required to go to school. Before Sam could drive off, he commented, "I have enjoyed your company very much. You have such a beautiful family, and I wish you will allow me to take you out again in the near future." With that, he drove off.

Evelyn could not understand why she felt like that with him. She felt so comfortable and relaxed like she had known him for a long time. That night, sleep eluded her as she kept thinking about him. *"What if he's a married man?"* He had never mentioned anything about his family or about his private life. *"What if he's just trying to be good…What if…oh, Lord, let me forget about him."* There were so many what-ifs that night, so many that they could fill a book. She turned on her bed, opened her eyes, and saw light streaking in her room, it was already morning. She could not remember how she had slept. She switched on the radio by her bedside and found a song, an old favorite love song. She was in no mood for love issues, she changed the station by tuning to another station where a popular gospel preacher was giving a sermon. Again she did not feel like being preached to …...She quickly turned the radio off, sighed, and lay back on her bed as she watched the day slowly begin to pass by.

Suddenly, her phone rang. Wondering who it could be, she reluctantly picked it up. It was Sam. She looked at the watch it was slightly after 0700 in the morning.

"Goodmorning. I just wanted to find out how the kids are this morning since they slept late last night." The truth was, he wanted to hear her voice because he as well had a sleepless night.

"They are fine, I think, though they are still sleeping."

"Have you had your breakfast yet?" he asked.

"Not yet. I am also still in bed."

"Sorry, didn't realize you could still be sleeping," he said apologetically.

"No, I have been awake for a long time. Couldn't sleep"

"Why?"

"Maybe it's because I slept late and my schedule was disturbed," she said as she pinched herself for telling a lie.

"Can I send you breakfast?"

"What! Please no, that won't be necessary." She hang up the phone, smiling to herself.

"Mum, you are making noise," Ali shouted from the other room; she didn't realize that she was singing on top of her voice. So it has happened; she only read in books that a person can do something without realizing. Here she was, acting the same. She laughed and threw herself on the bed. She had never felt so happy in a long time.

An hour later, a car hooted outside the gate. Thinking it was Sam, she went outside only to find a catering van.

"Goodmorning, ma'am, we've brought you breakfast." It was a full English breakfast. She was tongue-tied. This was way too much than what she expected. She felt like the sun was shining only on her and hoped that there should not be any rain. She went back to the house bewildered. *Do things like this happen in reality?* She wondered. She thought things like that only happened in fantasy books. She called him and again thanked him for the food. She further reminded him that he should not have gone through the trouble.

In answer, he said, "I kept you late last night, and I didn't want Ali troubling you that his breakfast was delayed." But it didn't end there; it continued for a long time.

To her dismay, Evelyn noticed that hardly a day passed without her kids mentioning uncle Sam. She wished she could stop them, but she realized that they missed having a father. Their father was dead, nothing could change that. She didn't want to get married again. She had inquired about Sam and knew that he was a divorcee, though she had noticed that he didn't like talking about his private life. She liked him though. But was liking enough to even make her miss him when he was not around or when he was not calling? It made her heart leap with joy whenever she saw him. Her dreams nowadays were so full of him. She was confused. She hated herself for allowing him to occupy their lives.

Yesterday, her life was a well-organized one. Yes, yesterday, she was a well-composed and principled lady, her life neatly planned. But since he appeared on the scene, all those qualities had vanished in thin air. Which road could she take to lead her back to yesterday where things where orderly and predictable? She wished she could find a way out, but somehow, she was enjoying the experience.

On Monday, she received a call from him, asking whether he should come to pick her up after work, to which she agreed. At exactly 1700 hours, Sam was outside waiting. The man was punctual. They agreed first to have a few drinks before going home even though Evelyn rarely took alcoholic drinks.

"Evelyn, do you ever think of getting married again?" he inquired. The question caught her off guard as this was the first time he ever asked a direct personal question.

She didn't know what to say but just blubbered that for now, she was comfortable with the status quo. She never thought about getting married again.

The way she said it made Sam laugh with tears in his eyes, he said, "You know what, sometimes you act so naive, I like the expression on your face, especially when you don't know how to answer. You should learn to hide your thoughts sometimes."

"I was trying." She grimaced "What about you? For how long have you been divorced, Sam?" She shot at him.

"I think it's about…uhmmm ten years now or thereabout."

"Why that long? Why did you let it take that long? Any plans of maybe reconciling with her?"

"Who do you mean her? Oh, you mean my ex-wife? No," he said emphatically. This time, he looked serious and explained that he's been divorced for over ten years."I told myself that I would never think about this ever, but I feel so comfortable with you. It's like I have known you all my life, Eve".I am not flattering you, but it's true. He continued, "I think I have come to like you very much. I have never felt like this for a long time…"He finished saying all this without her interrupting him.

Evelyn had become very quiet suddenly. She was touched not because of what he said but because she, herself, felt the same about him. It was like he was echoing her heart. She, therefore, decided to keep quiet lest she betrayed herself.

Sensing the silence he paused and asked "Aren't you going to say anything?."Anyway, even if you don't say anything, just know that your position in my heart is very important."

Evelyn knew that he could be lying, knowing his reputation… but the way he had said it made her heart melt. She looked straight into his big round eyes and said "Sam, You've said alot of things. and I appreciate to hear that I mean that much to you. Thank you very much, but honestly, I would rather we keep our friendship very simple let's not complicate things. Sam was disappointed to hear that but he still pushed on "I want you in my life Eve."

"I don't think I am ready for that. Please take me home." She said abruptly.

"I thought we came to have a drink…?" he asked, surprised at the turn of events.

"I am sorry, I think I need to go home now." She persisted. Quietly, without arguing, he turned the car. He sometimes failed to understand why women failed to handle the truth. Always wanting to postpone important issues! If it was any other woman, he was going to leave her, but this one—he didn't mind waiting even if it took one year for them to finish the conversation.

She didn't talk much on the way home, which made Sam start thinking that maybe he had offended her and hated himself for saying all he had said, but he could not help it. Perhaps it wasn't the right time now. What if she won't see him again? When he reached her place, he told her that he didn't regret saying all that he had said because that was how he felt.

She didn't respond, just got off the car, wished him good-night, and went into her home without looking back.

Her children saw her pale face and asked if she was all right. She lied that she had a terrible headache and just wanted to sleep. However hard she tried, she couldn't sleep. She fumbled for sleep like a drug that was difficult to find. Never had the refuge of sleep been more inviting, but it was not coming. She was surprised that she was behaving like a teenager on her first love. She knew if given chance, she could love the man, but she did not want to go that route. At work, she tried by all means to avoid his calls.

Her children at home knew something was wrong with their mother, and it made them unhappy.

Sam knew he was being avoided; a week passed without him succeeding to talk to Evelyn. Today he decided he was going to see her personally; no matter what she would say, he did not care. He was happy he had found love and he was not going to lose it for anything. He decided to go to her home in the evening. He knew that was the only place where he could not be avoided. He knocked on their door, and as usual, Ali came to open. "Uncle Sam," he exclaimed and jumped into his arms. "I missed you so much, where did you go?"

He couldn't answer, he laughed and lifted Ali up. He entered the house with Ali in his arms and found the sister watching TV. "Hi, Uncle Sam, long time," she said without turning her head.

"What film are you watching?"

"*Frozen*," She answered without the interest of getting into a conversation as she was so engrossed in the movie. He inquired if their mother was around. They informed him that for the past week, she had not been feeling well and thus she always went to bed early and never wanted to be disturbed.

He sent Ali to go and call her only to be told that she was fast asleep. He stood up and announced that he was going to see her in her bedroom. He knocked, but no reply came. He turned the knob, and the door opened. He went in and found her sitting on her bed, doing nothing in particular. He could see from her eyes that she was shocked to see him.

"Hi," he said.

"What are you doing here?" was the answer.

"I came to see you. I am tired of being avoided."

"Who is avoiding you?"

"It's obvious. Every time I call, there is always an excuse why I cannot talk to you. Why shouldn't I conclude that? I know you are not sick but just pretending to be. If what I said hurt you this much, I am so sorry, but I do not regret a single word I uttered."

"I hate you, Sam," she burst out crying.

Sam could not believe his ears. "What did you say?" he asked.

"I hate you for disrupting my calm life," she repeated with tears in her eyes. He drew near her, put his hand over her shoulders, got his handkerchief, and started wiping her tears. Whatever she would say, he would take it calmly, he thought.

"Sam, I am confused," she confessed. "I thought maybe by avoiding you, I would prove that I didn't love you." Upon hearing that, he heaved a huge sigh of relief. "But I think I was wrong". she continued. Because you haunt my life everyday, what can I do?" she asked like a schoolgirl stuck with arithmetic asking her teacher.

"Don't try to avoid what's inevitable. You cannot spend your life running away from the truth. Before you torture yourself any further, go freshen up we have to go and catch some fresh air."

"But the children…?" she inquired

"Don't worry, I will take care of that."

He went to chat with the children in the sitting room and announced that he was taking them out to his place. After a short while their mother entered the sitting room all dressed up. The children asked where she was going, but she just smiled. Sam looked at her approvingly.

"Okay, guys," he announced. "Let's go."

Evelyn felt nice for once to be controlled. She was so used to being in charge of everything; now, someone was in charge. It was a good feeling, and she kind of liked it.

Sam took them to his residence in Edenville Street. His house was beautiful, it had neatly cut lawns and beautiful flower gardens; it also had an amazing yard with neat driveways. They all just stood in awe of the place and could not believe their eyes. Evelyn had never been to Sam's house before and she never imagined that he stayed in such a beautiful house. It made her house in look like a ramshackle. The place had a high wall fence with guards all over. He instructed one of the maids to take care of the kids and give them food and whatever they wanted and further instructed them to show the kids to their rooms. It was all a dream for Ali; he pinched himself several times to make sure that this was real. He had never seen so many maids in one house and at the same time; only in movies. At their home, they could not afford even a single maid! The sister on the other hand was taking it calmly, recording every detail to be later narrated to her friends and especially her sister.

Sam and Evelyn left the children and went out to celebrate their reconciliation. They had their dinner over a candlelight. This brought back to Evelyn memories of her first date with her late husband. But nothing else mattered now, only Sam. She blossomed under Sam's attention like a flower long starved for water and sunlight.

They were listening to soft music played by a live band when Sam proposed marriage to her. Evelyn was shocked because that was the last thing she expected from Sam. It was like Sam enjoyed giving her surprises and she wondered how many more surprises were in store.

"Will you marry me, Eve?" he implored while taking out a shiny round thing.

Evelyn didn't need to think about it; "Yes Sam I will marry you" she said. Sam took the ring and placed it on her fourth finger. All that she vowed to herself didn't matter anymore. All that she wanted now was just to spend her life with him. Who cared about the vows of yesterday? Today needed to be enjoyed; no shadows from yesterday would be allowed to spoil the moment.

"I want us to get married as soon as possible". He announced. I don't want to lose you again" He sounded desperate, but who cared? Whatever he said was okay with her. They had the whole night to themselves to celebrate.

"Lukundo, don't you want to write a letter to Njavwa? I am writing to her now so you might as well write her", Evelyn instructed her younger daughter. In her letter, she enclosed a photo she had taken with Sam.

She sealed the envelope, with a smile on her face as she fixed the postage stamp.

5

Ring, ring, ring—the sound of the bell went, and immediately, everyone started packing their books, and noise erupted at once. The pupils were conditioned in such a way that whenever the bell rang, even if one was in the middle of a sentence, they had to stop reading.

Evening reading time, which was called prep, was over, and there was pandemonium everywhere. Mwaka and Njavwa packed their books as well and started going back to their dormitories, chatting and laughing like everyone else.

"Njavwa, you are hard-hearted, you mean you can keep an unread letter from afternoon up to now?

"Even me. I don't know why I don't want to read it now. But you know mum's letters are long and special so I want to take my time to read it. I will read it at bedtime."

And for sure at bedtime, she got the letter from under the pillow and lay down on her bed. She tore the envelope; and a picture fell out.

"Who is that?" Mwaka inquired curiously

"I don't know. It should be Mum's friend." Then anxiously, she started to read.

........Study hard. I have big plans for you when you complete school. I also want to inform you that I will be getting married. And the date has already been set in two months' time. I hope you will not receive the message with mixed feelings especially that we will get married without you. By the time you will be closing school, we would have shifted to Northrise, which will be our new home. That's your new dad, the man on the picture. His name is Samuel Kabwe.

Take care of yourself.....

The words on the letter became blurred; she could not finish reading the letter. Njavwa felt like she could die."No, it can't be... no, it can't be," were the only words she could utter, and everything went black.

"Njavwa, what's wrong?" Her friend panicked.

She picked up the letter thinking there was some bad news. After reading through the letter, she could not find anything that could make her friend pass out. She ran to call the other girls who also inquired about the news in the letter. They were astounded that the letter only contained good news of Njavwa's mum getting married. They could not understand why she had fainted. They rushed her to the sick bay where the matron on duty practiced her first aid techniques, to resuscitate her, but to no avail. The matron then suggested that she be rushed to the main hospital. The distance between the school and the hospital was about 7 kilometers but unfortunately, she was told that the school bus had broken down. During the night, it was very difficult to find transport, especially that the school was in the outskirts of the city. There was nothing they could do but just decided to wait and see.

When Njavwa came to, she found herself surrounded by people; she was confused as she couldn't remember what had happened.

"What's wrong, where am I?" she asked, looking confused.

Someone answered, You are in the sick bay. You have been sleeping for two hours now."Another added, "You fainted." The sick bay was a mini clinic for students, where they were treated for minor ailments.

The matron was relieved to see that Njavwa had woken up and looked fine. She then asked the other girls to leave so that they could give her chance to recuperate. She hated having to care for sick people because it inconvenienced her programs. She sometimes wondered why she agreed to take up the role of a school matron.

Early in the morning, Njavwa's friends went to see how she was doing; they found her asleep. As if she sensed their presence, she opened her eyes looked around the room as if she was trying to locate something. The eyes came to rest on Mwaka trying to ignore the others.

"What am I doing here?" She had experienced a great shock such that her mind blacked out and she had to be reminded what she was doing there.

It struck her as to why she had fainted, and she started crying uncontrollably. Everyone was puzzled; they did not know what was wrong with her. The matron decided that they leave her alone for some time till she calmed down.

Njavwa wished the world could come to an end. She wished the earth could open and swallow everyone, not just her alone; she didn't want to die. If only wishes were horses…

The matron came back after she had calmed down. She asked her how she was feeling. Njavwa couldn't answer because she didn't know how to describe how she was feeling.

"Njavwa," she continued, "do you have an idea of what made you faint?"

She lied that she just wasn't just feeling well. Njavwa hated herself for telling a lie, but how could she narrate her situation to anyone? The doctor came and did a thorough checkup on her and found everything normal.

Mwaka took the picture that had fallen from her friend's letter, looked at it for a long time. The couple on the photo was smiling at the camera and they looked happy. *Njavwa's mother is beautiful*, she thought. She picked up the letter for the fourth time that day. She read it again. Samuel Kabwe. Wasn't that the name of a person supposedly her real dad? It could be him.She had never met her real dad before, but her mother had told her that her father stayed in Ndola.It never bothered her since her stepfather cared and loved her just like his real daughter.

Mwaka wanted to know her real dad. She promised herself that she would hunt for her dad when she completed school. She put the photo in her bag.

What had made Njavwa faint? She wondered. Was there anything behind that letter? Njavwa never hid anything from her. Mwaka was very sure her friend would explain.

Njavwa was discharged from the sick bay two days later, and she resumed her normal lifestyle routine. However, her friendship with Mwaka was somewhat shaken. They both felt a small wall building between them. None, however, took the effort to break it before it grew higher. Njavwa was content because it was to her advantage. Life continued flowing like a river with no obstacles but with a lot of islands underneath.

Mwaka hoped her friend would explain to her what had disturbed her so much as to make her faint; she did not want to push her but decided to give her time to explain things on her own. Mwaka was mistaken because Njavwa had no intention of starting the story or narrating anything to anyone. Njavwa also was afraid that her friend was going to quiz her but prayed that she didn't and therefore remained withdrawn from everyone.

Mwaka could not keep her peace any longer. She had let the sleeping dogs lie for a long time; this time she was going to wake them up no matter how much trouble she stirred. She did not care. After all, Njavwa was her best friend; she had the right to know anything about her.

"Njavwa," she began, "I didn't realize you were sick that day. The way you fell you scared the wits out of me. You never told me what was wrong."

Njavwa had anticipated this coming, eventually the dreaded moment had come, but how was she going to explain her situation to anyone. *Should she tell her*? She debated within herself. "No, she might tell someone else". Njavwa trusted Mwaka with all her secrets but with this one…She didn't trust her enough. This secret was safe only with her alone.

"I really don't know how to explain because…er…I just found that I had fainted." She stammered . She knew that her friend was not buying her story, but she did not care.

"Njavwa, you are lying."

"Well, if you think I am lying, then what do you want me to tell you?" she retorted defensively.

"Okay, does it have anything to do with the letter or rather with your mum getting married?"

Njavwa grew scared that her friend had gotten closer to the truth. If she wanted, she could figure it out by herself, but the fact was she was not going to tell anyone.

"What makes you think it has anything to do with the letter?". "Look, I don't want to talk right now, okay?"

Mwaka noticed that the expression on her friend's face had changed. She decided to drop the subject and changed the tone.

"You know what, Njavwa, I don't know what to think. Do you know that the name Samuel Kabwe….."

"Look, I want to study," she rudely interrupted her friend before she could finish the sentence or hear what she had wanted to say.

Mwaka was taken aback with the reaction because her friend had never acted that way before. She became silent for a few seconds, trying to take that in then said, "If you don't want to talk to me, then well and good," and stormed out.

Njavwa knew she had offended her friend, but she could not help it. What was her friend trying to tell her about that name? "I wish I had not cut her short so that I could have heard what she wanted to say." she thought. Anyway, the less close she was to people, the safer the secret was with her. She tried to pick up a book, flipped the pages, but found that she could not read anything. She flung the book on the floor and threw herself on the bed. Perhaps dusk would show the way, but the darkness did not bring any relief. Even though she squeezed her eyelids shut, she could not avoid to imagine what lay ahead. She tossed and tossed, opened her eyes, and saw that her friend on the other bed was sleeping soundly. The whole school was quiet; the full moon outside shone as if it was in the room. The wind outside did nothing but kept her awake and reminded her of the letter and the photo below her pillow. She covered her head with the blanket and tried to pray. But she could not start.

She thought she heard someone say something and listened attentively only to hear her own breathing. She turned.

In class, Mr. Muntanga, her teacher, noticed that something had changed about Njavwa. She had become aloof lately. She was usually a witty and very alert student, but lately, she spent half of the time in class engrossed in thoughts. Njavwa was a natural active participator in discussions. However, lately she rarely participated in anything; she had just retreated in a shell. Something was seriously going on. He had tried inquiring from her best friend Mwaka, but she was equally in the dark like him.

That day, Mr. Muntanga was teaching biology. As usual, Njavwa was not paying attention as she was lost in her own world. As if in a dream, she felt Mwaka poke her with her elbow. "Njavwa, he's talking to you,"she whispered.

"Yes, madam, can you repeat what I just said?"Njavwa had no idea what he was talking about. According to her, she never heard him say anything.

"Njavwa, Iam talking to you. Can you repeat to the class what I said?"

"You never said anything, you were just moving your mouth, but your voice was not coming out." she said stupidly and the rest of the class burst into laughter.

"You see, class, don't think you can come to my lessons to daydream about your boyfriends. I am sorry I will not allow it in my class. This is your final term, and you ought to be serious," he said while rubbing his palms. Njavwa felt so humiliated. If only he knew what she was going through. Then as if shells were removed from her eyes, she saw the teacher for the first time in a different light. He was looking funny with a tight shirt and one button hanging on a thread wanting to fall, it was resting on his pot belly like a spiderweb. His trousers were short, reaching slightly above the ankles. He reminded her a cartoon character she loved to watch when she was a kid. Laughter choked her throat as she tried to suppress it but could not. She could not control herself. The whole class, not knowing why she was laughing, also followed suit.

The tall fat teacher was puzzled."What's funny? Can you all tell me why you are laughing?" he demanded, but he just added fuel to the fire. He did the next best thing; he took the blackboard ruler and started hitting the table. The class calmed down.

"Now, can you explain what that was all about?" He was panting with anger like a frog that had just eaten a hot potato.

"Now you..." He pointed at Njavwa. "Since you started it, can you now explain what is funny?" Njavwa sheepishly looked down and murmured her apologies.

"If you cannot offer any explanation, can you march out of my class now?"he ordered.

She knew what that meant, but she did not care. Inside she wanted to burst with joy. It felt so nice to get into trouble. She felt like one weight was lifted off her shoulders. That was a good laugh she had had in a long time. It made her day.

The teacher went home thinking about Njavwa. The girl had changed lately. She wasn't the same girl that he knew. She had been behaving strangely and stupidly recently most of the time. He tried to figure out what could be the problem and concluded that maybe she was having family problems of some sort. He would be watching her closely.

"How was the exam, Njavwa?"

She turned; it was him she knew it. He was always watching her. At first she thought he was after her, but she proved herself wrong. He was just a curious and nosy creature, that was how she described him. Lately he's been stalking her. "The paper was fair." She responded

"Have you passed?"

"I hope so."

That was the last exam paper she was writing for completing her high school. But was she really glad that she was going home? She did not know. The other students and her friends were excited shouting and jumping and singing.

"At last we are going home for good," Mwaka exclaimed excitedly and hugged her friend. "How does it feel to finish school? Wow, I can't wait to join the working class. You know—" She cut short the sentence after she realized that her did not share the dream, she did not look excited. Mwaka reached out her hand to Njavwa's as they walked toward the rooms in silence.

"You don't look happy," Mwaka commented.

"I am happy, but I am just not excited, that's all,"

"C'mon, Njavwa, we are going home after seven months of not seeing our families. At least there is a reason of being happy.

Can you imagine that?" Mwaka bubbled excitedly.

Little did she not realize that her friend's plans had gone with that letter she received. She was afraid of tomorrow because she didn't know how to face it. Njavwa was content with today; she didn't want it to go.

Mwaka knew something was terribly wrong with her friend. If only she could confide in her like always. They shared everything. As far as she was concerned, there were no secrets between them. Unfortunately, each passing day, her friend seemed to grow more and more distant. Mwaka tried to dig what her friend had buried, but to no avail. In the end, she just gave up and waited. Njavwa only talked when she felt like nowadays; she was no longer the bubbly friend she knew.

Mwaka wondered why her friend was dreading to go home. Now that it was time to go home, she still did not look excited about going home, though she was trying to hide under the disguise of someone missing home. Mwaka knew that was not true. Never in her wildest guess could she tell or even be near the truth to what was wrong. They say time reveals all things as there was nothing hidden under the sun. Indeed whatever it was would be revealed in due course.

Mwaka promised that she would give her friend a very big surprise. A surprise? No, a rude shock. "*First, let me go home and confirm with my mother. Then I will arise and set forth to Ndola,*" she thought to herself with a big grin on her face. She couldn't wait to see Njavwa's face when she would stand at their door and tell them that she had come home to Daddy. *Ndola here I come. Truly life is a funny story with a lot of crooked chapters each day revealing mysteries. I am going to write a movie*, she promised herself.

6

Finally the day of parting came; the head teacher addressed all the pupils that were completing school and wished them well in all their future endeavors. They bade farewell to each other as the booked buses came to take them each to their destination. Some students though had their parents picking them up. Parting always brought tears to the eyes especially after spending five years together, the students had developed a bond that became difficult to break.

Mwaka's time to go also came as the Lusaka bound bus arrived .They hugged each other and promised to be in touch with each other. Finally, the bus departed; the girls waved to those that remained as they waited for their transport to come. After everyone had gone, Njavwa remained alone with her arms around her shoulders as if she had lost something very dear to her life, and two big tears flowed down her cheeks. She was not crying because her friends had gone but was mourning for herself for what lay ahead of her. She felt pity for herself.

The sun suddenly grew scorchingly hot as if it was laughing at her. She looked at the sky, put her hand over her head to cover her eyes. Couldn't stand the heat she moved her bags in the nearby shade and sat on top of her biggest bag.

She didn't know what time the so called driver was coming to pick her up. All her friends had left, and she was one of the last few people remaining at the campus. It was so quiet, and she felt lonely. Her mother had rung the headteacher, telling her to wait for a car that was coming to pick her up. She was almost tempted to jump on the public bus but thought twice about it. *My mum would be disappointed*, she thought because she had sounded very excited when she was telling her that she was sending a driver to pick her up. She waited for almost two hours before a car finally showed up.

The thing was, she did not know the person who was coming to pick her up let alone the type of car it was. So whenever a car pulled over the car park, she would rush there to inquire who they were looking for, only to find that it was there for a totally different business. She lost the patience and now just sat down and started counting the ants passing on the ground. Another car, a gray Hilux, stopped in the car park. This time she didn't even pay attention when the man was asking for her name. She did not even see a person pointing in her direction. She just heard someone say hello. She turned her head to a man standing behind her clad in jeans, a colorful T-shirt, and fancy boots.

"You must be…aaah…Njavwa." Before she could answer, he continued, "I am Sandie," extending his hand. She took it in her palm and shook his hand. "I have come to take you home", he announced as if she didn't know the reason he was there."Is this all your luggage? Let's move it," he said, taking the largest case, and she followed suit.

"What took you so long to get here? You were supposed to be here by midmorning and this is past midday. I almost started to think that no one was coming for me" She complained. Sandie had to think fast because if this girl went to complain at home, he knew he would be in trouble.

He had started off in good time from Ndola. He delayed himself in Kapiri the next town when he had to stop to see some friends."Well…

er…," he stammered."I was detained by the traffic police on the way. You know the traffic cops are very troublesome. They thought I had stolen this vehicle, so they had to detain me for a while, can you imagine?"He hoped that he sounded convincing, and for sure it worked.

"Oh, I am sorry about that," Njavwa said sympathetically. "But how did they release you?"

"Well, after checking, they found that they were wrong, and that's how they released me."

"That was silly. Did they apologize?"

"Yeah, actually, they did."

"That's better, and hey, how is my mother?"

"Well, she's fine. Actually, you look so much like her."

"Oh."

"Yes, and I think you are much prettier."

She smiled. She liked him. He was easy to get along with.

"Is…is Mr. Kabwe home?"She inquired. She wished he could answer that he was dead.

"Mr Kabwe? You must be joking. It's time you started to call him Dad."

"He's not my father," she retorted. The driver turned his head sharply and stared at her; he was surprised at the change of tone in her voice.

"I am sorry," she said guiltily."I didn't mean to sound like that." And was relieved to see his face relax.

"No problem. Actually, he's been gone for almost a week now. He went abroad to the Uk, and I think he will be there for a month or so."

"Is that so" she said as she gave out a very big sigh. Again, the driver was puzzled.

"It seems like you don't like him, do you?"

She had to be careful before she made a fool of herself before this stranger.

"And have you met him before?"

"No…I can't wait to meet him." She pinched herself for telling this lie. It looked like it had become a habit to lie nowadays. She so much wished she could tell someone the truth.

They moved all the way to Kapiri without encountering any traffic roadblock. Sandie thought the girl had noticed that but Njavwa never noticed anything as she was lost in her own world. He looked at her and was tempted to ask what she was thinking about but, on second thoughts, just kept quiet. He stepped on the accelerator, and the car began to fly. At least he had gotten away with that lie.

Again, Sandie turned his head to look at his passenger and was greeted by her snoring; she was fast asleep. He put on the music he liked listening to when on the road, hip hop. He turned up the volume to full blast and stepped on it. If there was a way of monitoring drivers who polluted the road with noise, he was sure he would have been the first one to be caught. He changed gears as he whistled to the music.

Sandie had been a driver for the Kabwe Empire for seven years. He knew Mr. Kabwe liked him because he was efficient, humble, and trustworthy. There was never a time he had regretted working for Mr Kabwe. Only today because he had met his stepdaughter; had he met her in a different situation at another place, he definitely was going to make a hit on her. But if he knew what was best for him and his job, he should not even entertain those thoughts…

Sandie was the only driver who was assigned to special and private duties. Special duties included going with his boss wherever he went on his business trips. He was the only driver who would borrow a car for his private business. His friends envied him and he knew it and made sure his friends knew indeed he was special. Now that Mr. Kabwe was married, he was the only one who would drive his wife or kids when he was away on business like he was now. Mr. Kabwe never liked anyone driving his family, especially his wife; whatever he thought could happen to them only he knew. Sandie got along very well with

Mrs. Kabwe; he knew she also liked him. The secret behind his success was never complain, enjoy your work, be on time, and humble yourself. And surely it worked for him to qualify him into the good books of the Kabwe family and to qualify him to be the trusted driver among all the hundred drivers in the entire Kabwe empire.

When Sandie wanted to marry three years ago, Mr. Kabwe was his advisor and even helped him with some money to pay the dowry. Sometimes, he kept on wondering how his boss could give him the best advice ever when he himself was not stable where women were concerned. Especially that he knew most of his petty affairs. Maybe now he would settle down since he had decided to marry. He wondered what Evelyn did to convince his boss that she was the right candidate for the post. Especially that she even had three children.

Hence here he was today, assigned to pick up another child; he didn't know that she had another child old enough to complete school. So the new Mrs. Kabwe had three children in total! How did his boss arrive at marrying her when he had dated so many young women who had no children. How did he end up choosing a woman with children? That remained a puzzle not only to him but to so many other people.

He was curious to know the third child; he liked adventures, and he always related his trips to adventures. He enjoyed his work very much; perhaps that was what made him tick. He accepted his work as a challenge, and he felt very high behind the steering wheel.

Njavwa opened her eyes and looked outside the window, looked around, and asked, "Have we reached Kapiri?"While looking at her wrist watch.

"Yes, we passed it about thirty minutes ago, we are even about to reach Ndola now. You must have been tired the way you slept, I thought that maybe you have never slept for a long time."

She smiled."Yeah, we woke up very early, you know, the excitement of going home."

Suddenly, they saw the poster welcoming them to Ndola. As if reading her thoughts, he looked at her and said, "Welcome to Ndola." She lifted her eyes and the words "Welcome to Ndola, the friendly city" hit her eyes. Njavwa knew the drama had now started. She looked at it as if she was seeing that billboard for the first time. She suddenly became quiet and fixed her eyes in front with a blank look on her face. There were so many questions she wanted to ask this man, but how to ask them was a big problem. She regretted having slept on the way because the time she had wasted by sleeping, she could have found out a lot of things about where she was going. Now it was too late.

Sandie wanted to say something but changed his mind when he saw the look on her face. *It looks like this girl is moody*, he thought. He wondered what was behind all those mood swings. He looked at her again pensively. A car behind hooted; he came to and realized that he was blocking it from overtaking,

Meanwhile, Njavwa was talking to herself, asking why fate was mocking her. Another car sped by with a lot of noise, which quickly brought her back from her thoughts.

Mwaka reached home in Lusaka at night and found everybody indoors. Rhodesville surburbs was unusually quiet that night specially that the ground looked wet as if there were heavy rains during the day. She inhaled the fresh air of Lusaka. It was nice to be home after being away for such a long time. She felt happy.

Her family resided in the flats along Aggrey road. She knew her mum was already sleeping that time since she was usually an early sleeper. She couldn't wait to see the surprise on her parents' faces because they least expected her at that time of the night.

She knocked on her flat door. No response. She knocked again, then she saw lights in the kitchen come on. There were voices coming from the inside; no doubt they were wondering as to who would be knocking at that time."Who is it?" It was the voice of her stepdad.

"It's me," she answered

"Who is me?"

"Mwaka," she answered giggling.

'Mwaka!" he exclaimed, and immediately there was fumbling on the lock from inside. And no sooner had he opened the door than she jumped into his arms.

"Daddy!" she exclaimed.

"Why are you coming at this time? I have always told you that it's not safe to travel at night."She knew this was coming, and she was well prepared for it.

"Our bus had a puncture after Kabwe town."

"Poor baby, you must be very tired." Immediately, her mum appeared in the doorway in her nightdress.

"Who am I seeing?"she exclaimed excitedly."Mwaka, what a surprise! You are back," she said while embracing her."How are you, my dear?"

"Dinala!" she called her maid.

"Ma…"

"Come and help move this to the bedroom."She was referring to Mwaka's bags. Turning to Mwaka, she said, "How was your trip?"

"The bus had a puncture," answered her husband

Dinala showed up."Aaa…Mwaka, you have come, how are you?"

"I am fine," she said while shaking hands with Dinala.

"What are you waiting for? Carry these bags to the bedroom and make her bed. Is Anita already sleeping? Tell her that her sister has come."

"Let me carry this bag," Mwaka offered

"No, my dear, you are tired. Dinala will carry everything just go and greet your sister. You must be hungry let me run a bath for you so that you find the food ready, when you finish bathing then we can chat later."

Mwaka enjoyed this attention while it lasted, because she knew that just after staying for a week, they will be fed up with her. And the special treatment would cease. So she quietly went to her room while her mother went to prepare a bath for her. Mwaka felt like a queen being pampered. She found Dinala in the bedroom making her bed with Anita still fast asleep. Mwaka and Anita shared the bedroom. Dinala had worked for her mum for a year now but still feared her mum very much. Who wouldn't because Mercy was a no-nonsense woman.

Mwaka was even surprised to find Dinala still working at her place; she had thought that she would find her gone. She wondered how she had managed to work for her mother for a year now because other maids never lasted a month.

"You are still around."

"Yes, where can I go?"

"You have even grown fat, what have you been eating?" She laughed.

"You've come back with your teasing."

"Mmmmmmm…just tell me, is there a new catch?" Mwaka continued teasing.

"Ah you also", she responded shyly

Mwaka enjoyed a special relationship with the maid. They got along very well. She used to confide in her all the time because she could never bring herself to confide in her mum or her sister. She wondered what kind of mothers her friends had, because this one was a special kind who never joked with her children. She never saw herself telling stories with her mother. What kind of stories could they talk about anyway? .She remembered Njavwa narrating about how well she got along with her mother; she wished her mum could also become friendly.

Sometimes her mum used to rebuke her that she was getting too close to the maid for her liking.

"What kind of stories do you talk about? She's not your friend, not even your age mate." She would chide.

Mwaka then would just keep quiet because she knew if she argued, then she was putting Dinala in trouble. She avoided that at all costs because she understood her mum very well.

"Are you not going to wake your sister?"

"Oohh…," she said as she knelt down beside the bed and shook her sister. "Anita, wake up."

Anita opened her eyes and screamed, "Mwaka!" They hugged each other laughing.

"You are back, I missed you, It's so nice to see you, and you are here for good, I am so excited."

"Mwaka, your water is ready. Please go and take a bath before it gets cold," her mother called from the kitchen.

Days slowly passed, things slowly got back to normal. Her mother could bounce into the bedroom early in the morning to wake her up. The time of pampering was over, so there was no more special treatment for her.

"What kind of woman are you sleeping up to this time?" She would charge and Mwaka would grudgingly wake up. She knew when to answer and when not when her mum was talking. Every day was a day of lectures; when Mwaka and her sister tried to corner her to complain, she would answer, "Spare the rod and spoil the child. I don't want to do that with you."

"But, Mum, sometimes you overdo things. It's just too much…"

"Eh… eh… eh…Mwaka, just because you have finished school doesn't mean you have grown wings and you can control me. You are still under my authority." There was no joking with her mum, she was always serious.

Mwaka had always suspected there was something behind these daily lectures she used to receive from her mum. The treatment her mother used to give her and her sister was different. One day, Dinala commented, "Do you know that your mum treats you like you are not her daughter? At least your sister is treated much better."

She had noticed that too, but she thought her being the eldest was the reason her mum was too harsh on her.

She remembered a long time ago when her mum narrated to her that a man they were staying with was not her real father. It had started when one maid her mother had employed was asking why she was so different from the family. It never dawned on her as to why until another maid also noticed the difference and mentioned it. Unfortunately, her mum heard the comment and it didn't sit well with her. The maid was blasted and fired that same instant for meddling in issues that did not relate to her work.

However, that made Mwaka even more curious. She also joined in asking why her mum had chased the maid without a good reason. Until eventually her curiosity was satisfied when her mum narrated to her about this man she had loved very much. She explained how they met feel in love and immediately married. Their marriage could not survive because the man was always travelling as he was a businessman. He owned a lot of businesses abroad and property, so he was always travelling and obviously met a lot of other women. Just after five months, their marriage was on the rocks and it could not survive. The marriage could not continue any longer; she left. After some months, she discovered that she was pregnant. Thinking that the man would be concerned and call for reconciliation when he discovered that she was pregnant, he was never concerned. She was hurt but despite all that, she never stopped loving him. He had told her that he did not want anything to do with her again probably because he was already with another woman. If she needed money or anything it would be delivered to her the following day enough to take care of her and her unborn baby. That's how the chapter with that man was closed, never to be opened.

Then she, by divine fate, met this other man who didn't care that she was pregnant and agreed to marry her and care for her unborn child just like his own. She agreed though she knew in her heart of hearts that she would never forgive the real father of her child. She was still bitter that the other man didn't make any effort to reconcile with her. When the baby was born, she was exactly the picture of her father. Had she been a boy, she was going to be his twin.

"So that is the story of my life with your father. Since you were born, he had never bothered to find out whether you are alive or not. He cut every contact with me, meaning he doesn't want to have anything to do with you at all.

"I want you to never think of him, because as far as I know him he doesn't want to be bothered by you. Your father now is this man who has raised you up, who loves you like his own. So I don't ever want to hear about this issue again."And she emphasized, "Never should Anita or your father hear about this conversation, ever! Do you understand?"

All she could do was just nod her head after hearing the shocking news.

As she remembered all this, she understood that since her mother said she loved this man very much, maybe the way she was treated sometimes was just one of the ways of indirectly getting at him since she knew she never ever could have him. *Now, is it my fault that I look like him? I shouldn't pay for someone else's sins*, she thought to herself. What was surprising to her despite all was the fact that her father never mentioned or gave any indication that she was not his real child or tried to show it in any of his actions. Sometimes he bought things only for her, and her mother would protest, and he would be surprised because it never crossed his mind that he was segregating over any of their children. He loved his children the same; to him, they were all his.

She remembered how they had gone to a club with his father and then he started boasting and showing her off to his friends. "Meet my firstborn child," he would boast. When one of his friends commented that he had a beautiful daughter, he beamed with delight. Mwaka could even see the pride on his face, and she felt good.

One day, Mwaka went to visit her friends without getting permission from her mum as she thought it wasn't necessary. Immediately she stepped back into the house, her mother started; it had to take his father to intervene.

"No, Mercy, you are being too hard on this girl. Hardly a day passes without you nagging her."

"I am her mother, and I know best," she would answer.

"But is that the way you yourself was brought up?"

"That was a different generation," she would retort embarrassingly, realizing her mistake.

"Girls, let's go and get some fresh air. Your mother talks too much," he beckoned to the girls whilst grabbing his car keys

They would go for a ride which meant buying pizzas or delicious cream doughnuts at the food complex then finally would head back home.

In times like this, she wished this man was her real father; he was an angel. In real sense he was. Had her mum not mentioned it to her, she would never had a slight idea that she was not his real daughter. It hurt her to think that one day and not very far away from now, she would have to leave and hunt for her real father.

Surprisingly, she found that through it all, she never took offence when her mother was waffling. She had come to accept her the way she was. She tried to pretend that all mothers all over the world were like her own, which made it easy for her to accept her. She still loved her despite it all. But she could not imagine her reaction when she will announce that she wanted to meet her real father!

7

"um…Mum…Njavwa is here!" shouted Ali as he scampered toward the vehicle carrying her sister. Njavwa disembarked from the car smiling as she walked over toward him. He was running at full speed and threw himself into her outstretched arms with full force that she stumbled backward, wanting to fall. Chuckling, she hugged him, lifted him, and spun around with him in her arms. She pecked him on the cheeks as he was giggling and finally placed him down.

"Ooh, how you are, little brother? Is Mother home?"

"Yes." He nodded vigorously.

Suddenly, her sister also emerged from the mansion, went straight to bump into Njavwa, beaming with smiles. "Welcome. I missed you."

"Missed you too," she said as they hugged each other. "Is Mother home?" she asked again

"She's in the house."

Njavwa noticed something different about everyone. They were all glowing and clad in expensive clothes. If it was in the olden days, she was going to make a comment, but she was a changed person now. She had a lot of important pressing issues on her mind to comment on trivial matters. A curtain from one of the windows was drawn, and there was her mother peering. Suddenly, she felt a big pang of guilt in her heart, without having the power to stop it. She didn't know how to face her mum. The moment she saw her, she knew that things would never be the same between them.

She couldn't believe the transformation. Njavwa stood spellbound as she watched her mum walk toward her. She felt like she was Cinderella this time, everything around her was changing except for her.

"Njavwa, sweetheart, how wonderful to see you," She said, beaming."And how you've grown so thin, poor baby."Meanwhile Ali was busy tugging at her sister's hand and jumping around.

"Ali, could you leave your sister alone? She's tired," she scolded him jokingly."You see, Njavwa, how much you were being missed."Lukundo was walking behind them staggering with one of Njavwa's big bags.

"Congrats for completing school. I am so very proud of you."

.Njavwa's mum warmly wrapped her arm around her as she led her in the mansion.

From nowhere, maids in uniforms appeared and started to move bags into the house. Njawva had never seen so many maids in one house; she felt like she was watching a movie only this time, she was also in it, and worse still, she was the main actor.

The house was beautiful! She watched around her in silent amazement.

She was more than glad to have a room to herself for the first time as all her life, she had to share a bedroom with her young sister.

A surprise welcome party was organized for her in the evening, and few close friends were invited. She was touched by the thoughtfulness of her mother. She knew how her mother always did everything to please her. She was honestly touched.

It was good to see old friends after a long time; for once, she forgot all about her troubles and gave herself away to the excitement of the atmosphere. There was no doubt everyone enjoyed themselves. There was good music, exciting games, dancing, and enough food for everyone. It was nice while it lasted.

In the morning, as per usual habit, her mother came to her room to wish her a goodmorning. She found her already awake gazing in the ceiling."Good morning, you are already awake." Njavwa smiled thinly.

"How did you sleep?"

"Fine. Mum, thank you for the party, I really enjoyed myself."And for sure, she said it from deep down her heart.

"I am glad you liked it, but you don't know how proud I am that my first daughter has completed school. I can do anything for you, my child. By the way, how were the exams?"

"They were fair, but I can't say I passed," she said frankly

"No problem, dear, infact, I have already found a job for you. I don't know if you would want to start working now or maybe just go straight to college. It's up to you, but your new dad is arranging for a good university in the United Kingdom"

"Who is my father?" she interrupted. "I don't have a father."

Her mother was taken aback by that sharp reaction. It came so fast, she didn't expect it. She ran short of words as she looked at her with an open mouth.

"I am sorry Mum, it's just that I don't like it."

"What don't you like?"

She failed to answer but also didn't know what she meant by it.

"I just don't like the idea of you getting married."

"Is that so…?" her mum reacted."How can you say that? He is a good man," she said calmly. "Just wait till you meet him before you make your judgement, but I am sure you are going to like him." In her heart Njavwa agreed with her mum that those two days she had spent with him she had known that he was a good man indeed.

"Who wants to like him? Besides you couldn't even inform me and hear my views before you got married," she retorted sharply.

Her mum's temper started rising but quickly checked herself. "Since when did I start getting advice from you? I don't expect you to be talking to me like that…Okay, listen…," she said, trying to keep her temper in check."I know this came as a shock to you, but I thought it was for the good of everyone that I got married. Look how our life has transformed. Another important thing is that we love each other."

"You only think of yourself that's all. You don't even care whether we are happy or not", she snapped with tears falling down her cheeks.

"What is this hullabaloo all about? I don't understand…I thought about this very carefully before taking the step, infact I thought you guys needed a father."

"I don't need a father, I don't need nobody or anything from him."

"That's fine." Her temper rising again."If you don't need nobody, that's a very big problem because for as long as he remains the owner of this house," she said emphasizing her gesture with her hands, "he has to be respected."She emphasized, "And as long as I remain married to him, you have no choice but to call him Father."

"Why of all people did you chose him?"

Now Evelyn was confused."What do you mean?"

Failing to answer, Njavwa buried her face into the pillow, blocking her tears, which were coming out as if someone just unscrewed the nuts from a running tap.

"I understand you. I know you are used not to having a man around the house. I know every person would act the same way. But once you get used to it and accept the truth, it will be okay. And why are you crying? There is nothing to cry about here. Whatever is done is done, Njavwa, I cannot reverse things. Look, everyone including me is happy, so you better just accept that I am now married. Infact I am surprised. I thought you would be happy for me…" That's when big sobs where released.

Her mother was confused; she tried to soothe her, but to no avail.

She silently left the room and quietly closed the door behind her as she thought that maybe her daughter needed time alone to digest everything down.

From there, she ordered everyone to stay clear of Njavwa's room especially Ali, who had a long list of things to update her sister with. He had the habit of creeping into her bed in the mornings to go and tell her stories. This time, he had heaps and heaps of stories to tell. He could not wait, so when he woke up, scrambled out of bed in his wrinkled pajamas, sped past the corridors, and collided into his mother.

"Ali, where are you going? Njavwa is sleeping, and she needs to rest," she said firmly whilst holding his hand, leading him away from the door.

"But, Mum, I just want to say good morning."

"I know, sweetheart, but she doesn't need to be disturbed now."

"Mummy, just a little good morning."

"No, honey," she said, suppressing laughter.

"Okay, I will just open the door a little and then I…I just want to see her, Mummy, please just to see her, I won't even make noise then I will close the door, and then she won't even see me and then will go out, you hear me?" he said convincingly as he stopped walking and wanted to turn back.

"Now listen," her mum said as she tugged him again. "Immediately, you just open that door, you will disturb her, you understand?" She said, losing patience.

"Even just one peep?" he persisted.

"Ali…" Hearing that tone, he knew that he stood no chance of convincing his mother.

"Okay, Mum, I won't go in. I will wait for her to wake up and then I will go to see her," saying more to himself than to his mother.

"Now, that's my boy, off you go and change. Wash your face and brush your teeth while I fix you some breakfast."

This was a rare moment; once upon a time her mother used to

prepare all their meals. Since they moved in this new place, everything changed; she rarely even touched a spoon. The only time she would be in the kitchen is when she was preparing food for her new husband. Little did she know that the kids missed those moments when their mum would cook for them. Immediately he heard that she would prepare breakfast for him, he scampered away happily.

Whilst walking along the corridor, he passed by Njavwa's room. He stopped, thought for a moment, then started to walk away slowly; again, he stopped again looked back at the door, checked around, it was clear. He quickly went back opened the door quietly and entered the room. He stopped in his tracks when he heard sobs; he grew curious. He drew near. "Nja, Nja You are crying, what's wrong?" No answer. He stood for a moment then quickly left the room. He now understood why his mother had insisted on him not to come to this room. He didn't understand the reason Njavwa was crying.

He went back to the kitchen."Mum, what's wrong with Njavwa? She's crying."

"Who told you?"

He blushed; he knew he had been caught.

Looking down, he said, "I am sorry, Mum, but I just wanted to greet her. She wasn't talking to me…"

"Njavwa is not feeling well, that's why I said you should not disturb her."

"I am sorry, Mum," he said innocently.

"Okay, my dear, now come and have your breakfast."

"All right, I will be back. Let me just go and wash my face." And he scampered away.

Njavwa's condition did not change. She was not leaving her room; meals were sent to her room but came back untouched. The maids where gossiping amongst themselves wondering what was wrong with the girl. And speculations amongst them were high.

Njavwa's behavior did not worry her mother because she thought she was just upset about the talk they had the other day. But she was wrong; it continued for several days prompting the rest of the family members also to get concerned. As usual, Ali would go to his mum everyday and ask.

"Is Njavwa okay today? Can I go and see her? And Mum, she doesn't talk to me anymore, does it mean she hates us now?"he complained.

Her mum would reassure him, "Not at all, my baby. She is just sick. When she gets better, you will see she will start talking to you."Her mum also was trying to understand what really was going on. She wanted to understand the cause of the behavior change in her first child.

One day, Lukundo, her sister stormed on her mother

"Mum, have you noticed how Njavwa has changed these days?"

"Yes, I have."

"What is the problem?"

"I don't know, she's your sister. Please go and find out for me. Maybe she would tell you."

"But, Mum, she rarely comes out of her room, and when she does, she rarely talks to anybody in this house."

Her mother clicked her voice and clapped her hands in defeat."I really also don't know…"

Njavwa's mum decided to take the bull by the horns and interrogate her daughter again. She remembered how things were between them yesterday, how they used to laugh, joke, and talk about anything. How she was an easygoing child, so easy to love. How she used to tease her to start dating again. Yesterday, how she used to tell stories of everything happening in her life; she never used to hide anything. She really missed the friendship with her daughter.

I want my daughter back," she would cry.

Was her daughter hiding anything from her, or was it just the normal reaction of an overprotective child? She asked herself. She vowed to find out whatever the matter was.

"Njavwa, you haven't told me how your exams were," she started.

"There's nothing to tell."

What happened to the bubbly chatterbox? Njavwa was a girl who you just needed to introduce the topic of discussion and she would fly away with the conversation. Now this monologue conversation was not making sense. Surely something didn't sound right; something must be wrong somewhere.

"Do you know that your brother is very concerned about you? He says you don't talk to him anymore. You are not the Njavwa I know. What happened to you?"

"How do I act?" she asked trying to look innocent.

"You are asking how you act when you don't talk to people around here. Is there something bothering you, which you are not saying?"

She didn't respond.

"Then what is it? You are worrying me, and I don't like it. You need to confide in me. Remember, you can tell me anything. My getting married doesn't change the fact that you can still talk to me. Besides, your father will be away for one whole month, so we have all this time to sort whatsoever is troubling you."

Njavwa wished she could pour out her heart to her mother. She really needed someone to talk to, and she knew she was causing alot of anxiety to her family especially her mum, who seemed distraught. As much as she wanted to act normal, the guilt was weighing her down. It was like a very big load was on her shoulders. No matter how hard she tried to forget about it, the heavy weight kept reminding her that it was still there. She felt like going crazy.

She tried praying, but it was like the words where bouncing hard on her.

This time she gave up everything and just waited for the unknown to take its course. She remembered someone telling her that the present moment was never unbearable but what you thought was coming in five minutes or the next days is what drives you to despair. Somehow she acknowledged that it was true, but in her situation even the present situation was indeed unbearable.

"Mum…er…I wish I can tell you, but it's a bit complicated."

"What is it? Are you pregnant?" Her mum panicked.

"Nooooooo….., it's not that. Just give me time. I will say when the time is right."

Her mum was resigned.

Atleast she could see a little glimmer of light at the end of the tunnel, which was not bad at all for a start.

8

How will I face mother and daughter? Wondered Sam. Ever since he recognized the girl on that picture, his world had crumbled down. He was in a dilemma. He didn't know what else to do. He therefore decided to scamper to the UK where he had gone on the pretext of business. He was running away from the shadows of yesterday, which were pursuing him. What had he done? He asked himself countless times.

Ever since he got married, life was so blissful for him. He didn't realize that marriage could bring so much happiness in someone's life. His whole life had changed, and he regretted taking so long to marry. 'Indeed there can be no happiness equal to the joy of finding a heart that understands." The negative thoughts he had about marriage! Experience had taught him that marriage was an enduring companionship, which he could not keep up with. The heavens had smiled on him this time, what more could he ask for. Evelyn was such a perfect wife; how he found her it was only by divine connection. He didn't know perfect people still existed until he found this woman.

Sam was fulfilled.

They had such a strong bond like they were tailor made for each other. Sam didn't know that marriage could bring so much order in his life, and Evelyn didn't know she could find perfect happiness again. Heavens had indeed given them both a second chance. Evelyn knew from thereon that she could never ever want to be alone again. Everything in her life started revolving around this man. Samuel Kabwe was her world.

Samuel had assumed the role of father to Evelyn's children. He promised to take them all to good schools and make sure they never lacked. Samuel knew he had children outside this marriage; he didn't know if he could ever reconcile with them, but he found it easier to adopt Evelyn's children and make them his than to look for his flesh and blood. Life went on, and everything was as normal as could be.

Sam knew Evelyn's eldest daughter was at a boarding school, and he could not wait to meet her. He had heard so much about her. From what he had heard, she seemed to be an interesting and remarkable child. So whenever he was relaxing, he would ask his wife, "Please tell me more about Njavwa."

The wife would go on and on describing her to him. How she was an easygoing and likeable child. And she would flatter him. "You are such a great dad, she will also fall instantly in love with you!"

"You know, I can't wait to meet my 'firstborn daughter," he would brag. "You said you have some pictures which you haven't shown me, please bring them out I want to see them especially of my first born daughter." He jokingly requested his wife.

Njavwa was about to complete her high school education in a month's time, and Sam was getting anxious to meet the daughter he had never met. Evelyn went into her archives and removed all the photos of her family. She brought them to him.

"These are all the photos you need to see."

Sam started perusing through them one by one. Then as if struck by a bolt of lightning he stopped.

Suddenly, he remembered where he had seen this face.

"It can't be, no it could not be!"He had always known the girl was at Mkushi Girls, but he had never connected that she was the girl; he himself went to drop her there one day. It finally dawned on him why this family was so familiar…

His wife saw the husband's face suddenly losing color as if he had been struck by lightning.

"Honey, what's wrong? You look pale, are you okay?" She was alarmed.

"Yeah, er…er…am fine, I just need some water," he said while clearing his throat.

"Okay, let me bring it for you."

"No, I will get it myself," he said quickly as he stood up and headed straight to their bedroom door walking like a zombie. He was in shock

"This is not true, this can't be true!"he was muttering to himself.

Because of the way he stood up and the look on his face, Evelyn got concerned and followed him in the house.

"Honey, is anything the matter? You don't look fine."Evelyn knew her husband so well that there was nothing he could hide from her.

"Have you drank the water?"

Sam had forgotten the reason he had come to the bedroom. He was pacing aimlessly. She went closer to him and tried to feel his temperature; she thought maybe he had developed a fever.

He reacted sharply by pushing her away from him. She was shocked; she had never seen him like this.

Immediately, she knew something was very wrong. Sam could never raise a finger on a lady; he was a perfect gentleman. Now he had just pushed her.

Bemused, she quietly left the bedroom and went outside. She could not describe what had just happened. She thought Sam would follow her to apologize; but he was nowhere to be seen. The next she saw was the guard opening the gate and Sam driving out.

What just happened? She could not understand. What caused the sudden change of the mood? If he had received any phone call, she would have thought something had come up. But there was no phone call, no nothing; in just a blink of an eye, his mood had just changed. She decided to wait.

She was very sure he would come back and do the explanation of what was going on. They had promised not to keep any secrets from each other. That gave Evelyn the assurance that whatever it was, she would be informed.

When Evelyn got married to Sam, the first thing she did was to resign from her workplace. This was because she felt that she could not work with her husband's best friend as her boss. Sam was very happy when she agreed to resign because he didn't want his wife laboring to work. He told her that she didn't need to work for anything because he would provide everything she wanted. He even proposed to put her on a good salary just for being a full-time housewife. However, Evelyn had insisted that she didn't want to be a full-time housewife; she just had to find a job elsewhere. Sam had no problems with that either. He had agreed to allow her to look for a job though grudgingly; he didn't want his wife to work for anybody.

Samuel continued to be a good husband to his wife and a great father to Evelyn's children. Samuel found himself wishing that any one of his children with other women would come to stay with them. He was sure Evelyn would make a very good mother to them. But he didn't know where to start from, nor did he know how to contact any of the many women with his children. He never thought at one time he would need them. This was when he felt the need to be with his real children. If only he had kept in touch with them; he wished he could have them now since now he understood the importance of family. Life was full of twists. Look at him—before he didn't want to have anything to do with his children, but here he was, looking after someone else's children.

When Sam drove off from the house, Evelyn got the phone and tried to contact him to find out where he was going, but Sam was not picking up. She tried so many times but he wouldn't pick up, she eventually gave up. Sam never left the house without saying where he was going. This now really worried Evelyn. Was there a storm brewing somewhere?

That evening, Sam, who was normally home by 2000 hours was nowhere to be seen past midnight and his phones went unanswered. Evelyn could not sleep, she could not even eat as the feeling of apprehension started to get the best of her.

Suddenly, she saw her husband staggering in the bedroom. He could not even stand straight, and he was reeking of alcohol.

"What is this! You mean you were drinking?" She could not believe her eyes.

He mumbled something she could not hear.

He staggered over to the bed and fell face-first straight on the bed, and immediately he was fast asleep.

Evelyn just stood there and watched helplessly; everything was happening so fast. Sam drank? Whatever issue he had must be very grave, but what was it? She reasoned. Being a clearheaded wife, she walked over to where her husband was sleeping, removed his shoes, rolled him over to his side, and covered him.

Sam was already lost in dreamland.

The next morning, he woke up very early looking very sober and unusually quiet. He refused to have breakfast and just asked for a strong cup of coffee, which was given to him, and off he went to the office.

Sam was in a predicament. He didn't know how to face Evelyn or how he will face the girl. Suddenly, the world became too small for him. He was lost looking for a way out of his situation. Shadows from the past were creeping up on him. How could he escape this? Was there a way of shutting up the future. Yesterday seemed to be more comforting; he was not ready to go to the future, and he dreaded every minute that counted. He needed to come up with a plan and fast.

He called his travel agent and booked a one-way morning flight for the following day to England. That was his only escape.

He called his wife and asked her to pack for him as he would be travelling on an urgent business trip to the UK the following day. Shocked at the sudden unplanned trip, she tried to inquire when he would be back. She was even more shocked when she was told he would be gone for a month.

"A month!"

"Yes, sweetheart, cause I have to attend to some issues in England, and then I may proceed to France from there."

"So you mean you didn't know about this trip all this while?"

"I have just explained that there's an issue that has just come up, which needs my urgent attention."

Evelyn knew when not to push issues. She kept quiet and proceeded to perform her wifely duties.

When Sam had left the house in the evening the previous night, he had gone straight to his favorite drinking joint in the city. Usually he would go there to relax and interact with his buddies, but that night, he wanted to enjoy his own company. When he reached there he sat in the corner and ordered a beer. He didn't want to be in the bar as it was too noisy for him. He decided to call John to join him at the club. John sensed that something was not right by the urgency in his friend's tone on the phone, which made him not to waste time and quickly rush to where Sam was.

Because he was seated in the dark corner, John had trouble locating him. He kept asking where he was, and Sam, who was irritable already, explained a hundred times that he was in the last chalet in the dark. Finally, they located each other. John could notice that his friend was already drunk.

"Hey, what's up?"

"Am in a deep mess."

Startled, John asked."Is it Evelyn?"

"No, no no no, I am just in a deep mix of things right now."

"What have you done this time…?"

"My man, it's not me this time but my past sins…"

"Okay, don't keep me in suspense please, can you let it out?"

"On one of my trips to Lusaka, I met this girl and I gave her a lift. She was going to Mkushi, but I first went with her to Lusaka then I later dropped her in Mkushi at school."

"You mean she was a schoolgirl!"

"Yes…No…you…let me finish…She didn't look young to me, and I only discovered she was a schoolgirl after I had asked her."

"So? What's the issue…?

"Today I just discovered that that same girl is Evelyn's first daughter."

"Wha…what!" blubbered John, almost choking on his drink.

"My friend, am in a mess."

John then realized how serious the issue was. Sam never admitted that he was in a wrong, no matter what he did. The fact that he was willingly admitting a mistake meant it was beyond him. "You know I don't do that anymore." He continued."Please don't condemn me cause am guilty as charged. I just need your advice on how to handle this mess. Otherwise, I am finished."

John still in shock said, "Mwana, I don't know what to say, but I can agree with you that you are in deep trouble."

"What do I do? How can I handle this?"he asked simultaneously.

"Uhm…when is the girl coming?"

"She's writing her final exams, and she should be back in a week's time. I need to find the solution now before she comes."

"Does Evelyn know?"

"Are you kidding…no! But after today, she will know that something is up."

"Okay, cool down…Right now you need to go very far away, run. Come back after you have cooled down."

"Where do I go?"

"Go anywhere, somewhere…"

Why didn't he think of that before? "My man, am on the first flight to England tomorrow thanks to you!"

"Yeah, I think for now just go away until we figure out how you are going to handle the issue."

His friend was shaking his head, lost for words. That's why he loved John; he was sharp and very smart. He was grateful for this friendship. After having some more drinks and some serious chatting. John looked at his watch and suggested that it was time to call it a night. Sam refused; he didn't want to go home.

"Look, Sam, your phone has been ringing nonstop, meaning your wife is worried about you and the fact that you are not picking up…you need to go home now…"

"Okay I will go, but not just now…"

"Be a man, Samuel, you can handle this."

"Okay, my man, you can go. Let me just drink two more then I will go."

"No, I am not going to leave you here. We are leaving here together and now."

"What's the time?"

"It's now midnight."

"Okay, boss, since you insist…"

John settled the bill and walked his friend, who visibly had taken too much to drink, to the car. He made sure that Sam started off before he could also drive to his home. He told him that he would call when he reached home to make sure that he was safe. John was worried about Sam. His friend always ran away from problems—that had been his nature. He had no guts to face problems head-on; he always found excuses for his elusive behavior. This time, there was no running away; he needed to sort out the mess he had created.

Life was so full of mysteries. How could it be that after his friend had decided to settle down then this…? So was the saying, *"What goes round comes around was really true after all !* There was no running away from the past. It will always come crawling back to you until it found you…

Life.

Sam arrived in England in the afternoon and went straight to the hotel where he was booked. He needed to rest. He needed a long rest. How he wished he could travel with his wife. If it was under different circumstances; this was going to be the ideal place for their honeymoon, which they never had.

Sam had invested heavily abroad; he was a major shareholder on some major businesses in the UK. He had also invested in a number of properties abroad, which were giving him a good return on his investment. He decided to stay in a hotel for a week then he would shift to his apartment in the suburbs since he was not sure how long he was going to stay in England.

He called his family to inform them that he had travelled safely and was now just settling down. Whilst there, he decided to look at other investment opportunities that he could venture in. Once a businessman, always a businessman; Sam liked to maximize every opportunity that came his way. Maybe that was the reason he was branded a business tycoon in his own right. "That will keep me busy for the period that I am in exile," as he called his trip. A self-imposed exile indeed.

John was intrigued at Sam's story. It fascinated him so much that he was sure if his friend was a Hollywood actor, he would have been very famous. His lifestyle was just out of this world. He was tempted to narrate Sam's story to his wife but thought against it. Women, you can never trust them with anything sensitive. He therefore decided to keep the story to himself.

John had Sam's roaming number, which he used to communicate with him whenever he travelled out of the country. This time, he told himself that he would never call his friend to allow him enough space to sort out his life. Consequently, John took it upon himself to call Sam's home almost every day to find out how they were fairing in his absence. John was genuinely interested in their welfare, but he was also interested to know Evelyn's first daughter.

Whenever he called, he would ask if Njavwa was back from school. Evelyn finally confirmed that she had arrived on Friday and she was doing fine. Curiosity began to eat him so he decided to visit Sam's family to check on them. Evelyn was indeed grateful for John's concern as she knew that he was a part of their family. But whenever John visited, he would be told that Njavwa was in the bedroom. Until one day he asked why the girl was always in the bedroom. Evelyn could not resist but to narrate that ever since Njavwa came back from school, she never came out of the bedroom. She further complained that she had tried to find out the cause of the change in her daughter, but to no avail. She said she suspected the girl was hiding from something and now she didn't know how to handle the issue but wished that maybe with time things would get better.

John was genuinely concerned because he knew the cause of the girl's behavior. He suggested to Evelyn that he wanted to meet her, but Evelyn thought that it would not be possible as the girl might not agree. John insisted, and for sure, Evelyn called Njavwa from the bedroom, who reluctantly walked in dressed in her usual current attitude. John could not hide his shock as he looked at her; she was the real picture of her mother but in a smaller version.

Evelyn introduced them to each other. She explained that John was his former boss and also Sam's best friend. They were very close family friends. Njavwa didn't want anything connected to Sam, so just hearing his name made her frigid. John was very sensitive to that and explained that he just wanted to meet the "newest grade 12 graduate."For sure she didn't look interested; however, John finally managed to convince her to meet with him so that they could talk about her career prospects. So a date was set for Saturday in the afternoon.

Ali, who was listening silently, expressed interest in being part of the date and pleaded that he goes along. Njavwa wished Ali could be allowed to come along, but John blatantly refused saying he just wanted to meet Njavwa alone. And so it was.

Saturday finally arrived, and before coming, John phoned to confirm that the date was still on with Njavwa. He arrived slightly after midday, and thankfully, Njavwa was glad to come out of that house. She looked bright and said she needed to breathe some fresh air outside that house.

"Hi, uncle John."

"Yes, Njavwa, you look bright today. I will allow you to choose where you would want us to go."

"Jacaranda Mall," she suggested.

John refused he said he wanted something more secluded.

Then she told him to take them anywhere he thought best.

So being the driver, he decided to go along Kitwe Road to an Out of Town Resort. It is some modern resort in the remotest part of Ndola. It was about 30 minutes drive from the town centre. Njavwa was just wondering why he wanted to be in the bush instead of taking her to one of the nice malls around Town.

He chose a table under a tree far away from the crowd as the place was very crowded during weekends. It was a renowned good getaway from the hustle and bustle of town life. At least one could smell the fresh pure air from the bushes. A waiter came to their table to get their orders.

"What can I get for you?"

"A Fanta," she said.

And he ordered a Coke for himself.

"So, Njavwa" he began, "am sure you are wondering why I have brought you this far. There's a lot you and me need to talk about, and I didn't want us to be disturbed in the city," he began. "I hope you wrote your exams well."

"Yeah, I think so."

"That's good, but that's not the topic I want to talk to you about."

Njavwa was now wondering where the talk was leading.

"Your mum has been complaining that you have changed a lot ever since you came back. Do you have anything bothering you? Do you mind talking about it?"

Njavwa began to think this was her mum's plan of trying to make her talk. "There's nothing," she answered with a blank face

"Are you sure?"

"Yes, I am sure."

"I want you to be very honest with me. Do you have anything you would want to share with me?" John coaxed.

"Aah no… I don't thiiink sooo…" She rolled her eyes.

"Okay, at least I have something I want to talk to you about."

"Oh, okay," she said innocently.

"I know what happened between you and Samuel."

She almost jumped.

"Yes, I know why you have been behaving like that at home, and like I said, I know what happened between you and Sam."

She could not say anything; she just opened her eyes wide open in astonishment.

"Don't worry, at least your mum doesn't know anything yet." He emphasised.

She kind of relaxed a little, but she was still tense.

"Sam had told me everything about how you met and how you went to Lusaka and so on and so on…"

Njavwa didn't know what to do: to run or to hide or scream. She looked at him, her face devoid of any expression that John could not guess what was going through her mind.

He continued, "You are the reason you didn't find Sam at home when you closed school because he didn't know how to face you or your mother. But you can trust me, no one else knows about this except me. That's why I want us to discuss the way forward, which would be suitable for everyone so that no one could get hurt."

Njavwa developed a warm feeling toward uncle John and knew instantly that she could trust him. "I know my behavior at home is hurting everyone around me," she began. "But I don't know how to get out of this mess."

It felt nice to finally open up to someone. It was like one weight was lifted off her shoulder; she wanted to offload everything from her chest. "And I don't know if I can face Sam. And what if my mum finds out?."

"I know, that's why I wanted us to talk. What I want to do is this: I want to arrange for you to go away for a while. You can go and stay with a sister of mine who is a Catholic nun for a short while. I want you to go and reflect, I will handle your mother. I will tell her that you needed a retreat to think about your life. I feel you need a new environment. Is that okay with you?"

"Please…anything to get me out of that house!"

"Okay, I will make all the necessary arrangements."

She smiled. That was the first time he saw her smile. She felt close to John; he was like an uncle she never had. Finally, heavens had decided to send her help!

When Njavwa came back home, she was a completely a different person. She felt so high and she didn't realize she was skipping instead of walking, and singing instead of talking. She had never felt so light. Her mum and her sister, perplexed at the turn of events, just watched in amazement as she went around singing and mingling with everyone like before. They could not understand what had transpired in the date with Uncle John.

Her mum tried to find out what they had discussed at the meeting date with Uncle John. All she could say was he was just trying to find out what I wanted to do after school.

"And what did you say you want to be?"

"I didn't say 'because he asked me to take my time to think about it…"

"And…?"

"That's all."

"That's all?!" her mum asked bewildered.

Njavwa without caring about her mum's reaction continued playing "Catch me if you can" with her younger brother. She felt safe. Now at least she had someone to run to and someone who was watching her back. What more could she ask for?

"What happened?" Evelyn wondered. She could not believe that her real daughter was back.

Thanks to John and whatever he did."Thank you, Lord," she prayed with her hands lifted up, her face towards the heavens."Thank you for bringing back my daughter."

And so Njavwa was back. Everyone around her was happy. Njavwa had realized that she could not change the past; what she was just supposed to do was stop thinking too much, take the lesson learned, and move forward. She also learned that worrying never stopped the bad stuff from happening. It just kept one from enjoying the good. So she purposed to enjoy the present and let tomorrow take care of itself.

That was what she needed to do.

9

Mwaka was seated on her bed holding a photo in her hands. The man on the picture had big prominent eyes just like hers and she could feel the connection to him. It is said that people are born with five senses, but Mwaka knew she had a sixth sense. The sense came alive whenever she was not sure of something.

Mwaka had gotten the photo from Njavwa because her friend did not want to keep it. Njavwa was too carried away with her issues or maybe she really didn't care about the photo because she never asked about it. Mwaka was glad to keep it.

Njavwa's mum on the picture was smiling at the camera, she had Njavwa's smile. However, Mwaka's interest was not in Njavwa's mum but in the man beside her. So this was Samuel Kabwe...*Samuel Kabwe, my real father!* She wished she could show the picture to her mum, but knowing her mum, her reaction could trigger something else, which Mwaka was not ready to handle. She, therefore, decided to keep the photo right in her bag where only her eyes could see it. Every evening before going to bed, she could get the picture and gaze at it, trying to notice any more resemblance she could have with the man. In her heart of hearts, she was convinced this Samuel was truly her daddy.

Mwaka decided to embark on a mission: a fact-finding mission she dubbed Operation Find Daddy. Mwaka knew if she mentioned her plan to anyone, no one was going to authorize the mission. She kept all her plans to herself as she strategized on finding a way of travelling to Ndola. What was she going to tell her mum? She knew her mum's young sister stayed in Ndola, but they were not close and rarely communicated with each other. She really needed to find a good excuse that could convince her mum to allow her to travel. She had no problem whatsoever with her dad as he was an easy, flexible man, and she was sure he could never object. Her mum, on the other hand, was the exact opposite—so tough and rigid and unreasonable most of the times. Her parents were like the opposite sides of a coin—too different yet stuck together.

Mwaka decided to come up with the plan.

She started with her dad, as usual.

"Daddy, before my grade 12 results come up, I would like to go visiting."

"To where."

"Ndola, to Aunty Ruth's place."

"Why Aunty Ruth? Do you think your mum will approve?"

"Dad, you know when the results come out, I will be busy hunting for college places. I thought that its better I visit now before things get busy. Please, I just need a change of place just for a month or two."

George Musonda loved Mwaka like his own daughter. She was born in his house, and to him, that warranted her to be his child. George was naturally a very good man. He had a good job as an accountant in some big firm. He provided well for his family and ensured that they never lacked. Being a Christian and a leader in his local church had helped him to be the man that he was. George was a natural peacemaker and loved to live in harmony. However, his wife, Mercy, was the exact opposite. She was a quarrelsome person who always wanted to get her way in everything. George allowed her to get her ways most of the times for the sake of peace in the home. She was a complicated person that George used to wonder if all women were like her wife. He detested conflicts of any kind and therefore would do anything just for him to have quiet around him. They were so opposite in every way. Don't they say opposites attract?

George knew his daughter Mwaka was an intelligent, smart girl, and he also knew given the opportunity, she had great potential to reach far. Being the head of the family he took it upon himself to offer support to his family members in any way possible. On the other hand, Mercy didn't see much in her children and she was very tough on them. She never allowed them to have anything easy. It was like her intention was to break them, especially Mwaka; whatever her intentions were, George could not understand.

"Mwaka, I have no problem for you wanting to visit your aunt, but first, ask your mum and hear what she would say." Her mum had a final say on almost every issue. Mwaka eventually gained the courage to approach her mum when she noticed that she was in a relaxed mood after dinner as she was watching TV. She made sure her dad was around before asking.

"Mum," she began, "can I go to Ndola to Aunty Ruth's place?"

"To do what?"

"I just want to visit Aunty Ruth while I am waiting for my results its been a while since I last saw her. Can I?"

"Okay, Mwaka when do you want to go?"

"Over the weekend."

"You can go, but only for a few weeks."

"Thank you, thank you, thank you." She cried.

She couldn't believe that it could be so easy to get permission. Her parents had completely no idea why she wanted to travel to Ndola or what she was planning in her mind. Now that she had acquired the permission, how was she going to convince Kabwe that she was his daughter? She needed some empirical evidence of some kind. Her mother was the only one who could assist her, but getting through her mother was like climbing a wall. You really needed to have a lot of strength to push through; otherwise it was a futile exercise. Mwaka needed to make another plan to approach her mother. In the first place, she knew that should her mum find out why she wanted to travel to Ndola immediately, the trip would be aborted. So she needed to act very smart and that called for a lot of brainstorming.

Therefore the mission Operation Find Daddy was in motion. What did she need, her birth certificate? Her birth certificate bore the names of her stepfather; her real father's name was never put on any document. She was born Mwaka Musonda and not Mwaka Kabwe. Using the birth certificate was out. How about any picture? Had her mum kept any picture of her real dad by any chance? That was a million-dollar question.

She waited until when she thought her mum was in a jovial mood, timing was very cardinal in this matter. After dinner, her mum was packing some junk stuff in a spare room. Anita, her sister, was watching her favorite movie on Disney channel in the living room. Their father had gone for midweek service at church, and he usually took long to get back home. Mwaka's mind was racing. *Can I approach mum now?* She questioned herself. She finally gained the courage to make a move; she went to her and asked, "Mum do you need some tea? I am making mine, can I make you a cup?"

Her mum opted for coffee with cream. Mwaka made coffee for her just the way she liked it, with a lot of cream. Her mum got the cup from her and sat on a chair and started sipping the coffee. Mwaka again offered to help her mum with what she was packing—the old books and clothes, which she wanted to donate to charity.

"Mum, all this stuff…" She saw her old shoes and screamed, "These are my favorite shoes!"

"But you don't wear them."

"No, Mum, but I like them still."

"Learn to let go of things. Everything I have put here I am giving away because we don't use them."

After some silence, she started…

"Muum…Do you have any old photos?"

"What kind of photos?"

"I don't know…, anything like when you were a kid…how come you don't have pictures to show?"

Her mum smiled."No, Mwaka, our parents never used to take pictures of us."

"Uhm, how about any picture of my dad?" She held her breath,' she didn't know what the response would be.

"Which dad?"she responded not knowing what Mwaka was getting at.

"Like, my real dad…?"

Instead of getting upset, her mum burst into laughter. "Mwaka, I have told you never to talk about your father. Where is this coming from?"

"I am just asking."

"Okay, wait here, I will be coming."

You could see Mwaka doing a happy dance in her heart. She didn't know what to expect, but she knew something was happening.

Her mum went to her bedroom, brought down an old suitcase, which was stacked on top of the wardrobe. She opened it and took out an envelope. Her wedding photos fell out. She sat on her bed as she watched them one by one. This man. She had never loved anyone the way she had loved the man. Even she could not explain why their marriage could not last. He had told her that he loved her, but the way he changed when they got married…Deep down, she knew she could never stop loving him, and she had never stopped. But he had hurt her deeply. How love and hurt could be there at the same time, she could not explain. She had told herself that she did not want to have anything to do with him ever again and discarded everything that reminded her of him. However she could not throw away his pictures she had hidden them where her husband could never find them. Only she knew where to find those pictures.

She picked one picture and took it with her as she walked out of the bedroom. Mwaka was waiting in the other bedroom impatiently when her mum emerged."Here, this is your dad." She said as she threw a photo at her.

Mwaka grabbed the photo and looked at it for a long time.

So it was confirmed: this was the man "most wanted man"—Samuel Kabwe. You could see the excitement on her face.

"You see, I told you that you look exactly like him look at his eyes…"

"Can I keep it please?"

"For what, Mwaka? No, I don't want you to start developing ideas."

"Muuummy please…"

"Okay, if you promise to never show it to Anita or your dad.Is that understood?"

"I swear, I swear," she said excitedly.

Mercy never thought too much about it. She thought it was just the mind of a curious child and she saw no harm in showing her who her real father was.

"Thank you, thank you," she shrieked as she skipped out of that room right into her bedroom and put the picture into her bag. Her mum was left standing with a grin painted on her face.

Now Mwaka was ready to go.

That night, Njavwa could not sleep as she reminisced her conversation with Uncle John Phiri. She could not wait to leave town. Where she would go she did not care. What was important for her was to leave before her step dad came back from wherever he had gone. How could she face him? How would she face her mother? How could a man come between them just to spoil the beautiful relationship she had with her mother? What she could not understand is how the man convinced her mother to get married again. And how did she land on him out of all the men in the world. *That* was a puzzle she could not solve. There were so many questions than the answers she needed.

One thing she knew was that once she left that house there was no looking back. Wherever Uncle John was arranging for her to go, she would go. She would never step her foot in that house ever again.

From that day, Njavwa started taking one day at a time; she could not wait for the day she would stand on that door and bid good-bye to her family. She was willing to give up her life for the sake of her peace. She was willing to give up her family—that was the price she would pay for disobeying godly principles and going against her mother's teachings. She knew it was wrong to have sex outside marriage that the Bible was clear, but still she went ahead and did it anyway. She knew that now was the time to face the consequences of her actions. She thought she could get away with it, and she did—until now.

Everything had a price, they said, and the time to pay her price had come. She didn't mind living a lonely and dark life. "That's my cross," she convinced herself.

Now she wondered what Sam's cross would be; after all, he was the worst culprit here.

10

Samuel Kabwe's stay in the UK was eventually coming to an end. He felt that it was time to get back home because he thought he now felt ready to face the world. He therefore concluded his business and started getting ready to head back home. He had missed his family so much and he could not wait to see them again. His stay abroad had paid off as he had acquired more business deals and managed to establish links with other business houses similar to his. It was a worthwhile trip. Sam also took time to shop for his family. He found that he had more luggage than he had bargained for. It felt good to shop for his family as he spent most of his last days looking for things that he thought would please his family home. He didn't know whether all the stuff he had bought was necessary, but he bought them anyway.

Whilst abroad, Samuel had also taken time to reflect on his life. He knew he did not live like a saint, but that was long time ago. He was now a changed man, and he wanted to make up all the time he had wasted being a playboy. He was lucky to find Evelyn, the woman who understood him and did not intend to lose her for anything. He was going back to face his ghosts and fight them if need be."Yesterday, no matter what you bring today, you are never gonna ruin my life," he challenged life.

John had called him the other day to inform him about the plan to send Njavwa away. He explained to him that she was going to be sent to another province to stay with his sister, who was a Catholic nun at a convent. The girl had agreed to go without hesitation. The plan seemed perfect for Samuel because he didn't think he was ready to face Njavwa with her mother. John was so thoughtful; he thought about everything what would Samuel do without him? He promised himself that he owed his friend large. When he thanked him for coming to his rescue, all his friend said was, "I didn't do it for you, Sam, I did it for Evelyn so stop thanking me." But Sam was grateful anyhow.

Mwaka called Aunty Ruth to inform her that she had boarded a bus to Ndola and asked her to wait for her at the station. The bus usually took three and a half hours from Lusaka to Ndola. It was a tedious journey as the weather was hot and humid, blowing dry air in the bus. The air-conditioning system in the bus seemed not to be working which made the journey longer than usual. Everyone in the bus could be seen fanning themselves with hands or anything they could lay their hands on. Mwaka couldn't wait to arrive as the heat was suffocating her. The bus eventually arrived in Ndola.

She looked outside the window, and there was her Aunty Ruth, standing under a tall tree. Ruth, upon seeing the bus, started walking towards it. Broadway Bus Station was parked with people with all sorts of businesses and those that wanted to board the bus. As soon as the bus stopped, people started jostling toward it. Street vendors also joined in, trying to sell their merchandise to the passengers.

Ruth was the younger sister to Mwaka's mother. They never really resembled each other in any way. She was medium height and fat while her mum was tall and slender. She worked as a teacher at a secondary school. Ruth was a loner and never liked visiting; that's how come she stayed alone isolated from everybody. The two sisters were not very close and rarely communicated unless there was really need to. The children just wondered what kind of a family their mum came from.

"Aunty Ruth!" Mwaka screamed and waved from the bus. Her aunt spotted her and grinned. Mwaka came out of the bus and walked right into her auntie's arms as they hugged each other. They exchanged pleasantries, and she helped her collect her luggage, which was just a small suitcase, and took it to a car, which was parked right near where they were standing.

"Mwaka, how you've grown! How are your parents?"

"They are fine, and they send their greetings."

"Your mum allowed you to travel? What happened?" she queried curiously, because knowing her sister, she rarely allowed her children to visit any of their relatives unless it was really necessary. The children had grown up like that and never asked to go anywhere for holidays.

"Yes, she did. My mum has changed." And they both laughed knowing that that was not true. Aunty, do you still stay alone?"

"Yes, my dear, I think I am even used to my loneliness now."

"Why?"

"I just enjoy my company."

"Aunty, don't you feel scared?"

"You are here now, so there's nothing to be scared of."

Mwaka's mother's family were strange people; everyone had a weird character. They all had peculiar characteristics that were difficult to understand, but she understood them now.

After staying for a day, Mwaka remembered that she had not travelled to Ndola for nothing; she was on a mission. It was time now to resume her plan. First things first. She needed to get hold of Njavwa.

She had kept the telephone number for Njavwa's mum, so she decided to call her and inquire about her friend. She knew Njavwa's old home address, but that was before they shifted to the new address. She had no idea where they were residing now.

I will find them, she promised herself.

John Phiri had a long chat with Evelyn, trying to convince her to release Njavwa. He gave all kinds of reasons as to why Njavwa needed a break.

It would be better for Njavwa to go away for a while. He said Njavwa needed to be allowed to acclimatize to the transformation in their lives. He further assured Evelyn that he had an ideal place where the girl could stay for a while and reflect on her behavior. Evelyn listened to all John said, but she could not understand why John wanted to assume the role of guardian over Njavwa. "John, I appreciate all what you are trying to do for my family, but I think I know best what's good for my children."

"I know, Evelyn, but what I am trying to say is Njavwa's behavior had a cause, that's why it's better for her to go somewhere to compose herself for a week or two. I am sure after the break, she would come back a better person."

Evelyn tried to resist, but john convinced her. At the back of her mind, Evelyn still had a puzzle trying to understand why John seemed more concerned about Njavwa more than herself. In the end, John's will prevailed, Evelyn agreed that a week or two away from home would not hurt. Therefore, Njavwa was released. Besides, John had assured her that Njavwa would be very safe with her sister, who was a nun. Further that the environment in the convent was ideal for praying as well as a retreat for the girl who has been through so much trauma.

Evelyn was convinced that it was a good idea, and so a day was set for her travel. Njavwa was supposed to leave on Thursday while Samuel was due to be back on Saturday at midday aboard British Airways. He was scheduled to arrive in Lusaka then immediately connect to Ndola. John was expected in Ndola at slightly after midday since the flight from Lusaka to Ndola was about 45 minutes.

All was set for Njavwa's trip. However her mum wondered why Njavwa seemed so excited about the trip, which made her a bit uneasy. But as a Christian, whenever she felt like that, she knew what to do—get on her knees and pray. As much as she was dispatching Njavwa, Evelyn was also getting ready to welcome back Sam, who had been away from home for a month and half. She could not wait to see her husband as she had missed him terribly. She could not imagine how she had managed to stay without him for that long. She just loved him.

John called on their home on Wednesday evening unannounced, looking a little bit edgy. They thought he had come for his routine visits only to announce that Njavwa's trip had to be postponed because his sister had traveled away from her base and would get back after two weeks. Njavwa was crestfallen; it was like someone just popped her favorite ball. Her mind came to a standstill since she was all packed up and ready to go. She was at a loss not knowing what else to do.

Her mum was relieved because the trip had given her some discomfort and she did not have much peace at all. The fact that her child had to travel to Chipata and to a person she had never met before, she was not so sure. She was very delighted to hear that the trip had fallen off for now. The news was a like a drop of cold water in the thirsty ground. She quietly thanked her God because she had fervently prayed over it. To her, it was a confirmation that the trip was not supposed to happen. That's how Njavwa retreated to her cocoon again. There was no way out for her again. She was dejected.

Just after breaking the news, John immediately excused himself and left. No sooner had John left the room than Njavwa also immediately retired to her bedroom. The way she walked out…her mum and sister looked at each other with questions written on their faces. Njavwa had just turned into a person they no longer knew. They didn't understand why that trip meant so much to her. What was it that she was running to or rather running away from? Little did they know that Njavwa's shadows were slowly trying to catch up with her. She was making frantic efforts for it not to find her, but at the rate she was going, there was no escape.

Mwaka was resting in the lounge with her aunt. She had done the house chores and there was nothing else to do but watch TV. She remembered that she needed to find Njavwa. She picked up her phone and dialed Njavwa's mum. The number she got from Njavwa whilst at school. The phone was just ringing. She tried calling again, but little did she know that Njavwa's mum had forgotten her phone in the garden. The phone was lying on the flowers; it had slipped off Evelyn's pocket while she was taking a stroll in the flower garden. Evelyn loved flowers, and she loved doing rounds in the garden. She found so much peace by just seeing the flowers and inhaling their different fragrances. You could see her stop by one plant as if she was talking to it then move to another one just like that. That's how she spent her afternoons most of the time. She had no idea she had dropped her phone there.

Mwaka started getting desperate. If she did not get hold of Njavwa, then how will her mission be possible? She really needed to connect with her. Njavwa was the key to her finding her lost dad.

She tried to dial the number for the last time that day. A male voice answered. She was startled; she thought she had messed up the digits when dialing. The garden boy whilst tending to the flowers had found a phone right at the pavement and immediately recognized it to be for his boss. He picked it up and while he was fidgeting with it; it started to ring again. He started running to locate his boss and as he was running, he accidentally pressed the answer button.

"Hello, hellooo," he answered.

"I want to speak to Njavwa's mum." The voice at the end of the line said

He could not understand what the caller was trying to say. He ran in the house and found Evelyn in the lobby.

"Madam, madam your phone was ringing," he said, panting.

Evelyn picked up the call, but before she could speak, the phone had cut.

She checked her call log and saw a lot of missed calls from the same strange number. Getting curious, she decided to call back.

"Hello, someone was trying to call me from this line," she began.

"Yes, ma'am, my name is Mwaka. I wanted to speak with Njavwa."

"Which Mwaka is this?"

"Her friend from school."

"Oh…Mwaka, where are you?"

"I am in Ndola. I came on Wednesday."

"Oh really, that's great.Where in Ndola exactly."

Mwaka stated her location.

Just after talking to Mwaka Evelyn immediately developed an idea. She wanted to surprise her daughter; she thought having Njavwa's friend come over was going to be a good distraction to Njavwa's mood. Therefore she immediately decided to go and pick Mwaka herself.

"Can I come and pick you up right now?"

Mwaka never expected that. And Njavwa's mum sounded like she was excited over something. Maybe that's just how she spoke since she had never spoken to her before. She went in and informed her aunt that her friend's mother was coming to pick her up. She couldn't wait to meet Njavwa, and above all, to meet the man she had travelled for all the way from Lusaka.

The moment was finally here!

In about twenty minutes' time, there was a car at their gate. Mwaka, excited, thinking Njavwa had come ran outside to the gate—only to find Njavwa's mum alone.

"You must be Mwaka."

"Yes, I am." Mwaka was taken by the resemblance of her mum's friend to Njavwa. She looked exactly like the way she was on the photos, but she was even more beautiful in person

"How are you, my dear?"

"Am fine, ma'am."

"So who is at home with you?"

"My aunt."

"Can I talk to her?"

"Yes, please, you can come in."

She came out of the car and Aunty Ruth came out of the house to greet her. Evelyn had an aura of authority around her, making everyone feel intimidated. And she spoke with so much authority.

"I am Mrs Kabwe," she introduced herself. "And I have come to pick Mwaka. Is it okay if she spent a night at my place?" she asked.

"Yes, no problem, she can go," answered Aunty Ruth.

"Okay, Mwaka, please get your clothes. You will come back tomorrow."

Mwaka got in the car, and off they went to Njavwa's place.

"So how did you leave your parents?"

"They were fine, thanks."

"And how long are you planning to stay in Ndola?"

"Mum just gave me a month, so I should be going back at the end of this month."

"Oh, that's great."

"Is Njavwa around?"

"Yes, she is."

They reached the gate, and Njavwa's mum pressed some button, and the gate opened by itself. Mwaka could not believe what she was seeing. The place was beautiful. She didn't know she could find a such a beautiful house in Ndola. The house looked like a classy hotel.

*So this is where my dad stays…*She was speaking to herself.

Inside the house, she could not help but stare around as the place was a marvel to behold. It was awesomely huge.

"Ali," Njavwa's mum shouted. "Please come and greet Njavwa's friend. Where's Njavwa?"

"She's in her room," he responded.

"Okay please take Mwaka to Njavwa's room."

They walked through a winding corridor until they turned to a room at a far end of the long corridor. Ali stopped to knock. Someone answered from the inside of the room, and Mwaka opened the door.

"Njavwa!" Mwaka called.

Njavwa, who was engrossed in something, thought she was dreaming. That voice. She lifted up her head, and screamed at the top of her lungs.

"Mwaka!" she shrieked.

They ran into each other's arms.

Ali just turned quietly and left them. They didn't even notice that someone had left the room.

"Mwaka, what are you doing here?" her friend asked breathless.

"I came to surprise you," she responded, and she meant every word she said.

"What a good surprise, am so haaappy!" Njavwa screamed.

In her heart, Mwaka was not sure whether her friend would still be happy when she discovered who she really was! That did not matter for now, and they chatted away trying to catch up about the happenings in their lives. Mwaka indeed was a good distraction for Njavwa. Because of her friend, she forgot all about her problems and just became herself.

"Njavwa, your house is beautiful." Her friend couldn't help but comment.

"It's mummy's house, not mine."

"What do you mean mummy's house? It's yours too. I didn't know people stayed in beautiful houses like this."

Njavwa didn't respond as she listened to her friend praise the house.

"Please show me around," she continued.

"With pleasure. I will take you around Mummy's beautiful mansion," she said emphasizing the word *Mummy's*.

Mwaka gave her a friendly smack on her cheeks-,And they both giggled. They went around the house chatting and giggling. Her mum stood at a distance watching the girls giggling and holding hands. They didn't even notice that someone was watching them. So her initiative to bring Mwaka had paid off. She didn't like seeing her daughter troubled; she was happy only when her daughter was happy. She smiled to herself.

"Is your daddy around?" began Mwaka.

"Which dad? Oh, you mean Mr Kabwe." Retorted her friend.

Mwaka almost shouted, "My dad!" She restrained herself. It wasn't the time to say that yet.

Njavwa answered, "He left for the UK. I hear he's coming back tomorrow."

Mwaka's blood heated up; she could not wait to meet her dad. This was going to be the time of her life. So all this long, her dad lived like a king while she struggled with her mum! People who were not his children were enjoying his wealth while she, his real daughter, could not even afford a decent meal. Who could she confront to give her answers to so many questions that crowded her mind? So her dad was around and rich, and yet he had never bothered to find his family. How could he be comfortable with strangers when his real family could easily fill that gap? She couldn't wait to confront him.

She could not wait to see the surprise on their faces when she finally introduced herself as the real heir of the Kabwe empire. How will her friend react? she wondered. Little did she know that her friend also had a bombshell shocker waiting to be unveiled. Only time could tell which one of the shockers could scope the prize.

11

The plane touched down at exactly 11:45 hours at the International Airport in Ndola. His entire family had come to welcome the man of the house. Evelyn had made sure no one remained behind; even Mwaka was asked to come along. Njavwa tried to give an excuse to stay behind, but her mum would not even hear about it. Ali was ecstatic, jumping up and down; he had missed his dad.

Sam felt good to be back home especially to be back to his family. Is this what he was missing all the time he had stayed as a bachelor? He could never go back to that lifestyle again. He could never want to stay alone ever. He thought he had the best life before he married until he discovered that there was a better life. Indeed its true when it is said that you cannot miss what you never had.

Sam emerged from the plane feeling so carefree. He had been told that his problem, which had sent him scampering had been taken care of. But who was that girl standing next to his wife? Wasn't that the girl he was dreading to meet? What happened? He thought John had told him that he had taken care of business, what happened? He was getting more confused as he kept walking toward the exit. His mind was racing. Someone at least could have warned him that she was still there; maybe then he could have known what to do. He could have prepared his mind.

Where Njavwa was standing, she wished the ground could open up and swallow her before Sam could reach them. She didn't know how she would face him. Hence she kept fidgeting. Her mum was too excited to notice what was happening around her. Mwaka's heart was pumping like a racing machine. Finally, she was meeting the man she had waited all her life to meet. Her gaze was intently planted on him, trying to see whether the memory she had of him was real. The moment was finally here!

After being cleared by the airport authorities, Sam started walking toward his family with a grin on his face. He was holding his leather coat in one hand, a laptop bag on his shoulder, and pulling a hand luggage in his other hand. As he was walking toward them, Njavwa thought he was walking in slow motion with his eyes fixed on her. When he was just a few meters away from them, he clutched his chest and knelt down as if in pain. The things he was holding in his hand scattered about. As his mind was racing, his heart also starting racing thereby his blood pressure shot, causing the heart to malfunction. He collapsed. Emergency services were alerted; the medical team was there in no time, and before they knew it, the ambulance was wheeling at full speed to the hospital.

They were all confused, Things had happened so fast that they did not know what to do next. How Njavwa's mother jumped into that ambulance no one could remember; they just found that their mother had gone and they had been left, dazed.

Mwaka was very disappointed at the turn of events. She felt so frustrated; she had come this close to meeting her real father and this happened. Why at a time like this?

She became pensive and could not concentrate on any conversation. Meanwhile, Njavwa was in high spirits. She could not believe that it was possible for something like that to happen. Actually, if given chance, she would have started dancing right at the airport.

On their way home, Mwaka could notice that her friend was elated by something; she did not care that her father was in a critical condition. However, Njavwa's excitement could not even allow her to notice that Mwaka's spirit had fallen. She was reveling in the moment, and she wished that man would not come back.

They reached home, and Njavwa was in a celebratory mood. She put on some music and started dancing. Mwaka was appalled by the behavior.

"Njavwa, that is no way to behave when your dad is in hospital. Why do I get a feeling you are happy that your dad is in hospital?"

"Look, Mwaka, I don't care. That's Mum's problem."

Mwaka almost screamed that the man she was talking about was his dad. She controlled herself before she could say anything. These were the times she did not understand her friend. She sat down praying that the man would not die before he met her. She was really looking forward to meeting her dad. Who wouldn't want to know their parents anyway! She wished his condition was not serious so that he could come home soon.

Samuel's condition was critical. The nurses worked around the clock to bring down his blood pressure, which was not coming down.

"If he continues like this, he could develop a stroke," the doctor explained to Evelyn. "But we are trying everything possible to ensure that we stabilize his blood pressure." The doctor could not understand what was raising his blood pressure. They performed all the necessary tests to determine the possible causes of the problem;. All the tests yielded nothing. All they had to do now was wait and pray.

Right now, Sam remained unconscious, oblivious to what was happening around him.

12

The relationship between Njavwa and Mwaka became strained. They could not understand why they were pulling at each other all the time. Little did they know that they both had different interests in the man, which had made them to be at loggerheads. They had a cold war without realizing that they were fighting with each other. Each seemed to be so engrossed in their problems to discover that they were actually fighting.

Mwaka continued staying with them at the insistence of Njavwa's mother. She was more than glad to stay, and of course, even Njavwa was more than glad to host her friend. For Mwaka, it was like the jigsaw puzzle was slowly taking shape. What remained was just one big piece to complete the whole picture.

One morning, Mwaka confronted her friend."I have a feeling that you don't like your stepdad. Did anything happen between the two of you?"

Njavwa first laughed and then answered. "You are right, I don't like him one little bit. I wish he could stay in the hospital forever," she said frankly without realizing that she was hurting her friend.

"Do you know that that same man in the hospital could be my dad?" Mwaka approached the subject diplomatically.

"Yes, he's your dad if you want him to be," Njavwa answered quickly without understanding what her friend meant. She thought her friend was trying to make a joke out of the statement.

"Njavwa, what I mean is Samuel Kabwe is my real dad."

"You are joking."

"No, am not joking, Njavwa, I am serious. My mum told me about him."

"How? I mean are you serious?" Njavwa knew her friend had never met her real dad. She had grown up with her stepdad who she knew as her father. After seeing the seriousness on her friends face, Njavwa knew her friend could never joke on anything like this.

"What when did you find out?"

"I found out when you received a picture and a letter from your mum. It raised my suspicion, which was confirmed by my mum when I went home."

"But you never told me." She said accusingly

"I tried to tell you, but you brushed me off."

Njavwa remembered how her friend wanted to tell her something about Samuel Kabwe, but she never wanted to hear that name and shut her friend up.

"You see, I tried, but in the last days of school, you changed though you never told me what caused that change."

Njavwa felt so guilty. It was like her guiltiness was becoming heavier and heavier by the day. Making it even more difficult to confide in her friend.

"Does your mum know that you found your dad?"

"No, she doesn't, but I will have to tell her soon. She even gave me a picture of my dad. So you see, we are real sisters after all."She joked, and she continued."I am very disappointed that he's down right now because I can't wait to meet him. I want to know my dad, Njavwa," She said with a serious look on her face.

Samuel began to slowly show signs of improvement. At least he was able to open his eyes, but he could not talk yet. His faithful wife was always by his side, faithfully tending to him. The doctor assured them that if he continued like this, he could be on the road to recovery. Evelyn continued to care for him and encourage him to get better. She was always talking to him even if he was not responding, she was not getting tired of talking to him. Sam's medication was always on time, and he continued responding steadily. As the days went on, they discovered that Sam could not move his legs; he had developed a partial stroke. The left side of his body was paralyzed.

The news came as a shock to Evelyn, but she was counseled by specialized nurses who told her that paralysis could be cured. They explained that with the right medication coupled with physiotherapy, her husband could get well soon. They lectured her that she needed to have alot of patience because the recovery process would be very slow, but it was possible for Sam to be back to his old self again.

In time, Sam was released to go and recuperate from home. But he still could not talk and walk. He came out of the hospital in a wheelchair being pushed by his wife.

At home, Njavwa made sure she stayed as far from Sam as possible. She never went near where he was, and everybody just kept wondering what was with Njavwa. On the other hand, Mwaka was always nearby, caring for him. Whenever he needed something, Mwaka was always nearby. Sam was wondering where this girl came from, and he developed a strong liking for her. Whenever Evelyn was not there, he preferred Mwaka to be around him. She would take him around the yard in his wheelchair and kept talking to him and telling him to be well because she needed him more than anyone else. She needed him. Sam couldn't understand what she meant, but he knew that this girl was special. He couldn't ask who she was, but whenever he saw her, you could see his face lighting up the whole room.

Njavwa's mother noticed the bond between the girl and her husband. She took it as just one of those twists of fate. She was grateful that Mwaka was always there when Sam needed anything, and strangely enough there was a very strong resemblance between her husband and Mwaka. They both had same smiles and similar big round eyes. Evelyn never thought too much about it, just thought it was just one of those pure coincidences. Whenever Sam's friends came to see him, they would all comment on Mwaka as they mistook her for his sister or some close relation. The resemblance was so striking. *She's just an angel sent from above*, Evelyn would tell herself.

Njavwa could not continue staying in the same house with Sam. She discovered that whenever by accident she met him, she experienced feelings that she could not explain. She could not take it any longer. She knew deep down her heart that she loved the man. She could not continue like this any longer. She had to find a way for herself.

She went in her bedroom and locked herself there as she pondered on what to do.

She got a pen and a paper and began writing. She wrote a short note folded it nicely, and placed it on her bed. With tears in her eyes she packed her clothes in a small bag and went out through the back gate.

Mwaka is the one who discovered that Njavwa was missing. She noticed that her friend was nowhere in sight. Since all the time Mwaka was with Sam, Njavwa could be tucked in the house not wanting to come out. The only time they would spend time together was in the evening when Evelyn could take over looking after her husband. It so happened that Mwaka did not know what Njavwa was planning the time she was alone.

She checked the house, upstairs in the TV room; she went in the gardens—Njavwa was nowhere to be seen. She asked everyone in the house if they had seen her, but no one seemed to have noticed as she sneaked out of the house. She went in her bedroom and sat on the bed. As she sat there, she noticed a paper with big words written: MUM.

Mwaka picked the note, opened it, and read it. She did not understand what it meant, so she rushed out to look for Evelyn. "Ma'am," she called. "Could you please read this…?"

Evelyn read the note but she also could not make sense of it.

Dear Mum

I know you would be shocked to hear my confession, but I cannot keep it inside me any longer…I knew Sam when I was going to school. I went with him to Lusaka then he dropped me at school. He's the one who gave me a lift and bought me all the nice clothes, which I have .I cannot face my past and him and you in this house. The only way is for me to go very far where you cannot find me.

I love you so much, Mum, and I wish you well.

Pray for me always,
Njavwa

Her mum panicked, tried calling Njavwa's phone, but it was not going through it was switched off. She read the note again. *What does she mean and where is she going? It* suddenly, dawned on Mwaka what her friend meant. She realized that the uncle who brought Njavwa to school was actually her father, Samuel Kabwe. It also dawned on her why Njavwa had reacted like that when her mum was getting married and the apparent open hatred for Sam.

Njavwa's mother on the other hand could not take it. Her own Njavwa could not do that. There had to be some logical explanation somewhere.

"This is not real, it's not true. Let me call her again to explain what she means." Evelyn panicked. She called the number again, but it was switched off. The shock was too much for her to take. She could not sleep that night and she could not think straight. She kept pacing about like an insane person. She kept imagining where Njavwa could go because she didn't know anyone out there. Evelyn felt like her whole world was crumbling down on her. She knew her husband used to be a playboy, but she did not know to what extent. That's when it dawned on her that she knew very little of her husband's past; she never bothered to dig it. She had told herself that yesterday should remain in the past; there was no way she was going to start looking for the buried road of yesterday to discover what happened there. Her main concern was the future .But she was wrong; she underestimated the shadows from the past. There was no running away.

As she pondered over her predicament, she relived the memories when she was showing Sam Njavwa's pictures. His sudden reaction and how he had scampered to the UK. Everything now began to make sense. Things were falling into place. How he had collapsed at the airport—maybe it was because he saw Njavwa and could not face her. What Evelyn didn't know was that another shock awaited her when she would discover that Mwaka was actually Sam's daughter.

The next morning, Lukundo noticed that her mum was not waking up. She was usually an early riser but it was 0900 hours in the morning and her mum still was sleeping? That was very unlikely. Getting concerned, she went to the bedroom and knocked. No answer. She knocked again and called out her name, still no answer. She touched the door knob and opened the door. Her mum was sleeping soundly. She went nearby and kept calling her.

"Mum, mum!" No response. She tried shaking her, that's when she realized that her mum's body was lifeless.

Lukundo shrieked on top of her voice and ran out of the room. Everyone appalled gathered and asked what was wrong. She could not say anything. She was hysterical and just kept saying, "My mum, my mum." The maids ran to the bedroom, and for sure, Evelyn's body was cold. They rushed her to the nearest hospital. The doctor who received her examined her and immediately informed family members that the person was already dead. She was a brought in dead (BID) case. After some examination, the doctor observed that Evelyn had been dead for five hours, which meant she died in the early hours of the morning in her sleep.

That was a bombshell.

The people could not tell Sam what had happened because they were worried it could worsen his condition. John Phiri came in and took charge of the situation; he asked one of the drivers to take the kids to his home.

He asked everyone to be calm and not alarm Sam, who was not too well himself. He further instructed the doctor to do a postmortem to determine the cause of Evelyn's death.

Eventually, John had to take the courage and inform Sam of the death. When Sam learned of the death of his wife, his entire world collapsed. There was nothing for him to live for now. Again, he had nothing. He could not take it.

"Lord, why are you punishing me. Haven't I paid enough for my sins?" he cried. The heavens were silent; the skies were clear making it look like a blue blanket covering the top of the earth.

After the postmortem, doctors discovered that she had too much pressure on the brain, causing the arteries to rapture. Evelyn had died of shock.

There was nothing else left to live for. The kids could not understand what was happening around them. Their peaceful life suddenly had been rocked by disaster after disaster. Their sister had disappeared and no one knew where she had gone. Their stepdad was on a wheelchair with no sign of recovering soon, and now their mum—who was their pillar, their strength, their life—was no more. What was happening to them?

Just watching them cry could melt your heart even if your heart was made of stone. It was so painful. Ali was the most confused; he didn't know first why her mum had gone to the hospital. Njavwa had disappeared without a word. And they are telling him his mum would not come back...

Mwaka called her mum to explain that she was no longer at Aunty Ruth's place but was staying with Njavwa. At least her mum knew Njavwa was her best friend at school. And that Njavwa's mum had died in her sleep, so she would stay over until after the funeral. She didn't disclose to her mum that Njavwa's mum was married to Samuel Kabwe. That information for now was not necessary.

When Mercy heard about the funeral, she was touched especially when she heard how Evelyn had died. She felt sorry for the children. Out of genuine sympathy, she told her husband that she would love to travel to Ndola to fetch Mwaka and also to attend the burial of Njavwa's mum. Mwaka's dad encouraged her to go to the funeral and offer support to the family.

After the funeral, Sam called his family around and told them, "I know your mum is no more, but we have to learn to live together without her. You are my family and you are all I have now. It will not be the same I know, but we have to learn…....."And he broke down crying like a woman. He was inconsolable.

Sam again promised himself never to look at any woman again. This was the second time he was saying that after his first failed marriage and now after the death of his wife. He knew he was the cause of everything and only heaven could help him. He had caused the death of his wife. How can he forgive himself? Why didn't Evelyn wait for him to narrate to her the real story? Just thinking about it made him burst into tears.

They say time heals all wounds; but for him, not even time will manage to heal his pain. He was in real pain.

Mwaka and Ali tried to cheer him up, but he could not be comforted.

Mercy came to the funeral house, and Mwaka and Lukundo received her from the gate. She came in and started consoling the children and wished them well. She encouraged them to trust in the Lord because he was the only one who could take could care of them. She offered to be there for them should they need anything. By that time, Samuel was sleeping. So when he inquired about their father, the children told her that he was sleeping and he could not be disturbed.

It was getting late, and Mwaka's mum thought it was time to go back. She even told Mwaka to get ready as they would be leaving in two days' time. She was lodging at her sister's place in the nearby township. As she was standing up to go. Samuel entered, driving his wheelchair. It was the automated wheelchair sometimes he used to drive himself around. He saw a familiar face; he was sure this was Mercy, his first wife. What was she doing in his house?

As she was walking out, he called out her name. Startled, she stopped. She could never mistake that voice for anything. She turned. There he was in a wheelchair. At first, she didn't recognize him then…

He had changed. There were deep lines on his face, and she could see sadness in his big eyes.

"Samuel!"

Meanwhile, Mwaka had withdrawn, standing far, watching what could happen.

"Is it you?" Mercy was taken aback; she knew that the owner of the residence was Kabwe, but she never imagined that it was Samuel Kabwe, her Samuel. She retreated back to him, knelt down beside him, and hugged him as they both started weeping. They stayed like that for a long time. Both were weeping for many things that had gone wrong in their lives. After a while, Mercy removed her hands around him.

"Sam, my deepest condolences for the loss of your wife. I didn't know this was where you stayed. I came here because Mwaka and Njavwa are friends, so I came to offer my sympathies," she explained before Sam could ask anything.

"Mwaka, come here." Mercy called out.

Mwaka drew near.

"This was the girl who was born after I had left."

Mwaka could not believe that it was actually her mum who was doing the introductions. Sam, with his mouth agape, shook his head. No wonder he was taken to her the first time he saw her. Indeed it's true: blood is thicker than water. This was his own blood. He could not back his tears…

After Njavwa left the house that day, she went and slept at a guesthouse to plan her next course of action. She had saved a bit from the monies her mother used to give her. The money at least was enough to see her through until she reached her destination.

Life was done for her; there was no looking back. What was done was done.

How could she live with her mum in the same house?

The following morning, she got on the bus to Chipata in search of Uncle John's sister, the Catholic num. Chipata is a town in the farthest eastern side of the country bordering with Malawi. She knew the directions since she was given the first time she was supposed to travel. That was the only place she could hide.

When she reached there, the first thing she said was, "please enroll me into sisterhood."John's sister, who was already a nun, wasted no time in introducing her and registered her for sisterhood. Njavwa was later transferred to Mwami a border town between Malawi and Zambia where she continued her training as a Catholic nun.

Njavwa completely erased her life from her memory and never talked about it to anyone. She used to tell people that she had no family and her family was now the church. She told her mind never to think about her past. She could not contain the guilt that came from the thoughts. She therefore dedicated herself to keeping in prayers all the time that was the only way to run away from the shadows that were pursuing her.

Njavwa never heard about her mum's death; she didn't know that Mwaka now stayed with her siblings or that Samuel never regained his health.

No one heard from her again.